AGENTS OF LIGHT AND DARKNESS

SIMON R. GREEN

2003
50TH
ANNIVERSARY

ACE BOOKS, NEW YORK

THE BERKLEY PUBLISHING GROUP
Published by the Penguin Group
Penguin Group (USA) Inc.
375 Hudson Street, New York, New York 10014, USA
Penguin Group (Canada), 90 Eglinton Avenue East, Suite 700, Toronto, Ontario, M4P 2Y3, Canada
(a division of Pearson Penguin Canada Inc.)
Penguin Books Ltd., 80 Strand, London WC2R 0RL, England
Penguin Group Ireland, 25 St. Stephen's Green, Dublin 2, Ireland (a division of Penguin Books Ltd.)
Penguin Group (Australia), 250 Camberwell Road, Camberwell, Victoria 3124, Australia
(a division of Pearson Australia Group Pty. Ltd.)
Penguin Books India Pvt. Ltd., 11 Community Centre, Panchsheel Park, New Delhi—110 017, India
Penguin Group (NZ), 67 Apollo Drive, Rosedale, North Shore 0632, New Zealand
(a division of Pearson New Zealand Ltd.)
Penguin Books (South Africa) (Pty.) Ltd., 24 Sturdee Avenue, Rosebank, Johannesburg 2196,
South Africa

Penguin Books Ltd., Registered Offices: 80 Strand, London WC2R 0RL, England

This is a work of fiction. Names, characters, places, and incidents either are the product of the
author's imagination or are used fictitiously, and any resemblance to actual persons, living or dead,
business establishments, events, or locales is entirely coincidental. The publisher does not have any
control over and does not assume any responsibility for author or third-party websites or their content.

AGENTS OF LIGHT AND DARKNESS

An Ace Book / published by arrangement with the author

PRINTING HISTORY
Ace mass-market edition / November 2003

Copyright © 2003 by Simon R. Green.
Cover art by Jonathan Barkat.
Cover design by Judith Murello.
Interior text design by Julie Rogers.

ISBN: 0-441-01113-6

ACE
Ace Books are published by The Berkley Publishing Group,
a division of Penguin Group (USA) Inc.,
375 Hudson Street, New York, New York 10014.
ACE and the "A" design are trademarks belonging to Penguin Group (USA) Inc.

PRINTED IN THE UNITED STATES OF AMERICA

18 17 16—15 14 13 12 11 10 9

I'm John Taylor. A private eye who operates mainly in the darker areas of the Twilight Zone.

The Nightside is the sick, secret, magical heart of London, where gods and monsters go to make the deals and seek the pleasures they won't find anywhere else.

I find things. It's a gift. And sometimes . . . they find me.

ONE

Everyone Believes in Something

There is only the one church in the Nightside. It's called St. Jude's. I only ever go there on business. It's nowhere near the Street of the Gods, with its many and varied places of worship. It's tucked away in a quiet corner, shadowed and obscured, no part of the Nightside's usual bright and gaudy neon noir. It doesn't advertise, and it doesn't care if you habitually pass by on the other side. It's just there, for when you need it. Dedicated to the patron saint of lost causes, St. Jude's is an old, old place; a cold stone structure possibly older even than Christianity itself. The bare stone walls are grey and featureless, unmarked by time or design, with only a series of narrow slits for windows. One great slab of stone, covered with a cloth of white samite, serves as an altar, facing two rows of blocky wooden pews. A single silver cross hangs on the wall beyond the altar; and that's it. St. Jude's isn't a place for comfort, for frills and fancies and the trappings of religion. There is no priest or attendant, and there are no services. St. Jude's is, quite simply, your last chance in the Nightside for salvation, sanctuary, or one final desperate word with your God. Come to this church looking for a spiritual Band-Aid, and you could end up with a hell of a lot more than you bargained for.

Prayers are heard in St. Jude's; and sometimes answered.

I use the church occasionally as a meeting place. Neutral ground is so hard to come by in the Nightside. Only occasionally, though. All are welcome to enter St. Jude's, but not everyone comes out again. The church protects and preserves itself, and no-one wants to know how. But this time, I had a specific reason for being here. I was counting on the nature of the place to protect me from the terrible thing that was coming. From the awful creature I had very reluctantly agreed to meet.

I sat stiffly on the hard wooden seat of the front pew, huddled inside my white trench coat against the bitter chill that always permeated the place. I glared about me and tried not to fidget. Nothing to look at and nothing to do, and I wasn't about to waste my time in prayer. Ever since my enemies first tried to kill me as a child, I've learned the hard way that I can't depend on anyone but myself. I stirred restlessly, resisting the urge to get up and pace back and forth. Somewhere out there in the night, a force of destruction was heading straight for me, and all I could do was sit tight and wait for it to come. I let one hand drift down to the shoe box on the seat beside me, just to reassure myself it hadn't gone anywhere since the last time I checked. What was in the box might protect me from what was coming, or it might not. Life's like that; particularly in the Nightside. And especially when you're the famous—or infamous—John Taylor, who has been known to boast he can find anything. Even when it gets him into situations like this.

The dozen candles I'd brought and lit and placed around the church didn't do much to dispel the general gloom of the place. The air was still and cold and dank, and there were far too many shadows. Sitting there, in the quiet, listening to the dust fall, I could feel the age of the place, feel all the endless centuries pressing down on me. St. Jude's was supposed to be one of the oldest surviving buildings in the Nightside. Older than the Street of the Gods, or the Time Tower, older even than Strangefellows, the longest-running bar in the world. So old, in fact, and so long established as a place of worship that there are those who hint it might not even have been a church, originally.

Just a place where you could talk to your God, and sometimes get an answer. Whether you liked the answer you got was, of course, your problem.

It's only a short step from a burning bush to a burning heretic, after all. I try not to bother God, and hope He'll do me the same courtesy.

I don't know why there aren't any other churches in the Nightside. It's not that the people who come here aren't religious; it's more that the Nightside is where you go to do the things you know your God wouldn't approve of. Souls aren't lost here; they're sold or bartered or just plain thrown away in utter abandon. There are presences and avatars, and even Powers and Dominations, to be found on the Street of the Gods; and you can bargain with them for all the things you know your God wouldn't want you to have.

There are those who've tried to destroy St. Jude's, down the centuries. They aren't around any more, and St. Jude's still is. Though that could change this night, if I was wrong about what I had in the shoe box.

It was three o'clock in the morning, but then it always is in the Nightside. The night that never ends, and the hour that stretches. Three o'clock in the morning, the hour of the wolf, when a man's defences are at their weakest. The time when most babies are born and most people die. That lowest of points, when a man can lie awake in his bed and wonder how his life could have turned out so very differently from

what he'd intended. And, of course, the very best time
to make deals with the devil.

All the hairs on the back of my neck stood up suddenly, and my heart missed a beat, as though a cold
hand had closed fleetingly around it. I lurched to my
feet, an almost violent shudder running through me.
She was close now. I could feel her presence, feel her
gaze and cold intent turned upon me as she drew
nearer. I grabbed up my shoe box and clutched it to
my chest like a life preserver. I moved reluctantly out
into the aisle, and turned to stand facing the only
door. A single great slab of solid oak, five feet tall and
five inches thick, locked and bolted. It wouldn't stop
her. Nothing could. She was Jessica Sorrow the Unbeliever, and nothing in the world could stand against
her. She was close now, very close. The monster, the
abomination, the Unbeliever. There was a stillness to
the air, like the tension that precedes the coming
storm. The kind of storm that rips off roofs and drops
dead birds out of the sky. Jessica Sorrow was coming
to St. Jude's, because she'd been told I was there, and
I had what she was looking for. And if they and I
were wrong about that, she would make us all pay.

I don't carry a gun, or any other kind of weapon.
I've never felt the need. And weapons wouldn't do
any good against Jessica Sorrow anyway. Nothing
could touch her any more. Something happened to
her, long ago, and she gave up her humanity to become the Unbeliever. Now she doesn't believe in

anything. And because she doesn't believe with such utter certainty, all the world and everything in it are nothing to her. None of it can affect her in the least. She can go anywhere, and do anything, and she does. She can do terrible, distressing things, and she does, and nothing touches her. She has no conscience and no morality, no pity and no restraint. The material world is like paper to her, and she rips it apart as she walks through it. Luckily for the world, she doesn't leave the Nightside much. And luckily for the rest of us here, there are long periods when she just sleeps or drops out of sight. But when she's up and walking, everyone gets the hell out of her way. Because when she concentrates her unbelief on anything or anyone, they disappear. Gone forever. Even the Street of the Gods closes up shop and goes home early when Jessica Sorrow is abroad in the night.

Her most recent rampage had been one of her worst, as she stormed through all the most sensitive parts of the Nightside, leaving a trail of chaos and destruction behind her as she searched obsessively for . . . something. No one seemed too sure of exactly what that might be, and absolutely no one had any intention of getting close enough to her to ask. It had to be something special, something really powerful . . . but this was Jessica Sorrow, who was famous for not believing anything was special or powerful. What use could the Unbeliever have for material possessions any more? There was no shortage of objects of power in the Nightside, anything from wishing rings to description theory bombs, and every damn one of them was up for sale. But Jessica Sorrow would have none of them, and people and places vanished under her angry glare as she continued her rampage. The word was, she was looking for something so real she would *have* to believe in it . . . perhaps something real enough and powerful enough finally to kill her, and put her out of everyone's misery.

So Walker came to me, and told me to find it. Walker represents the Authorities. No-one really runs the Nightside, though many have tried, but the Authorities are the ones who step in and bang heads together whenever any of the movers and shakers look like they're getting out of hand. Walker is a calm and quiet sort, in a neat city suit, and he never raises his voice because he doesn't have to. He doesn't approve of lone operatives like me, but he throws me the odd job occasionally, because no-one else can do the things I can. And because as far as he's concerned, I am entirely expendable.

Which is why I make him pay through the nose for those jobs.

I can find anything. It's a gift. From my dear departed mother, who turned out not to be human. She's really not dead; that's just wishful thinking on my part.

Anyway, I found what Jessica Sorrow was looking for, and now it lay in the shoe box I was crushing to my chest. She knew it was here, and she was coming to get it. My job was to present it to her in exactly the right way, so that it would defuse her anger and send her back to wherever she went when she wasn't scaring the crap out of the rest of us. Assuming, of course, that I had found the right thing. And that she didn't just storm right in and unbelieve me out of existence.

She was outside the church now. The solid flagstones under my feet vibrated strongly, echoing to the tread of her approaching feet, crashing down heavily on the world she refused to believe in. All the candle flames were dancing wildly, and the shadows leapt around me, as though they were frightened too. My mouth was very dry, and my hands were crushing the shoe box out of shape. I made myself put it down on the pew, then straightened up and thrust my hands deep into my coat pockets. Looking casual was out of the question, but I couldn't afford to seem weak or indecisive in the presence of Jessica Sorrow the Unbeliever. I had hoped that St. Jude's accumulated centuries of faith and sanctity would offer me some protection against the force of Jessica's unbelief, but I wasn't so sure about that any more. She was coming, like a storm, like a tidal wave, like some implacable force of nature that would sweep me effortlessly aside in a moment. She was coming, like cancer or depression, and all the other things that cannot be denied or negotiated with. She was the Unbeliever, and compared to that St. Jude's was nothing and I was nothing . . . I took a deep breath, and held my head up. To hell with that. I was John Taylor, dammit, and I'd talked my way out of worse scrapes than this. I'd *make* her believe in me.

The heavy oaken door was reinforced with heavy bands of black iron. It must have weighed five hundred pounds, easy. It didn't even slow Jessica down. Her thunderous feet marched right up to the door, then her fingers plunged through the thick wood and tore it like cloth. The whole door came apart in her hands, and she walked through it like a hanging curtain. She came striding down the aisle towards me, naked and emaciated and corpse pale, the heavy flagstones exploding under the tread of her bare feet. Her eyes were wide and staring, as focussed as a feral cat's, and as impersonal. Her thin lips were stretched wide in something that was as much a snarl as a smile. She had no hair, her face was as drawn and gaunt as the rest of her, and her eyes were yellow as urine. But there was a force to her, a terrible energy that drove her on even as it ate her up. I held my ground, giving her back glare for glare, until finally she crashed to a halt right in front of me. She smelled . . . bad, like something that had spoiled. Her eyes didn't blink, and her breathing was unsteady, as though it was something she had to keep reminding herself to do. She was hardly five feet tall, but she seemed to tower over me. I could feel my thoughts and plans disintegrating in my head, blown away by the sheer force of her presence. I made myself smile at her.

"Hello, Jessica. You're looking . . . very yourself. I have what you need."

"How can you know what I need?" she said, in a voice that was frightening because it was so nearly normal. "How can you, when I don't know myself?"

"Because I'm John Taylor, and I find things. I found what you need. But you have to believe in me, or you'll never get what I have for you. If I just disappear, you'll never know . . ."

"Show me," she said, and I knew I'd pushed it as far as I could. I reached carefully down into the pew, picked up the shoe box, and presented it to her. She snatched it from me, and the cardboard box disintegrated under her gaze, revealing the contents. A battered old teddy bear with one glass eye missing. Jessica Sorrow held the bear in her dead white hands, looking and looking at it with her wild unblinking eyes, and then, finally, she held it to her shrunken chest and cuddled it to her, like a sleeping child. And I began to breathe once more.

"This is mine," she said, still looking at the bear rather than at me, for which I was grateful. "It . . . was mine, when I was a small child. Long ago, when I was still human. I haven't thought of him in . . . so long, so very long . . ."

"It's what you need," I said carefully. "Something

that matters to you. Something that's as real to you as you are. Something to believe in."

Her head rose sharply, and she turned her unwavering regard on me. I did my best not to wince. She cocked her head to one side, like a bird. "Where did you find this?"

"In the teddy bears' graveyard."

She laughed briefly, but it surprised me anyway. "Never ask the magician how he does his tricks. I know. I'm crazy, but I know that. And I know I'm crazy. I knew what I was buying with the price I paid. I'm always alone now, divorced from the world and everyone in it; because of what I did to myself, what I made of myself. La la la . . . just me, talking to myself . . . It wasn't an easy or a pleasant thing, to cut away my humanity and become the Unbeliever. I walk through the world, and I'm the only one in it. Until now. Now there's me and teddy. Yes. Something to believe in. What do you believe in, John Taylor?"

"My gift. My job. And perhaps my honour. What happened to you, Jessica?"

"I don't know, any more. That was the point. My past was so appalling, I had to make myself forget it, had to make it unreal, had to make it never have happened. But in doing that I lost my faith in reality, or it lost faith in me, and now I only exist through a constant effort of will. If I ever stop concentrating, I'll be the one to disappear. I've been alone for so long, surrounded by shadows and whispers that mean nothing, nothing at all. Sometimes I pretend, just to have someone to talk to, but I know it's not real . . . But now I have my bear. A comfort, and a reminder. Of who and what I was." She smiled down at the battered old bear in her stick-thin arms. "I've enjoyed our little chat, John Taylor. Made possible by this place, and this moment. Don't ever try this again. I wouldn't know you. Wouldn't remember you. Wouldn't be safe."

"Remember the bear," I said. "Just maybe, it can lead you home."

But she was already gone, striding out of the church and back into the night. I let out my breath slowly and sat down on the front pew before I fell down. Jessica Sorrow was too damned spooky, even for the Nightside. It's not easy having a conversation with someone you know thinks she's only listening to voices in her head. And who can drop you out of existence on the merest whim. I got to my feet and went over to the altar to collect up my candles. And that was when I heard running footsteps approaching the church from outside. Not Jessica. Human footsteps, this time. I retreated to the very back of the church and hid myself in the deepest of the shadows. Apart from Jessica, and, of course, Walker, no-one was supposed to know I was there. But I have enemies. Their dread agents, the Harrowing, have been trying to kill me since I was born. And besides, I'd had enough excitement for one night. Whoever was coming, I didn't want to know.

A man in black came running through the gap where the door used to be. His dark suit was tattered and torn, and his face was slack with exhaustion. He looked like he'd been running for a really long time. He looked like he'd been scared for a really long time. He was wearing sunglasses, black and blank as a beetle's eyes, even though he'd come out of the night. He staggered down the aisle towards the altar, clutching at the pews with one hand as he passed, to hold himself up. His other hand pressed an object wrapped in black cloth to his chest. He kept glancing back over his shoulder, clearly afraid that whoever or whatever pursued him was close behind. He finally collapsed onto his knees before the altar, shaking and shuddering. He pulled off his sunglasses and threw them aside. His eyelids had been stitched together. He held out his parcel to the altar with unsteady hands.

"Sanctuary!" he cried, his voice rough and hoarse, as though it hadn't been used in a long time. "In God's name, sanctuary!"

For a long moment there was only silence, then I heard slow, steady footsteps approaching the church from outside. Measured, unhurried footsteps. The man in black heard them too, flinching at the sound, but he wouldn't look back; his mutilated face was fixed desperately on the altar. The footsteps stopped, just at the doorway to the church. A slow wind blew in from the night, gusting heavily down the aisle like someone breathing. The candles nearest the door guttered and went out. The wind reached me, even in my shadows, and slapped against my face, hot and sweaty like fever in the night. It smelled of attar, the perfume crushed out of roses, but sick and heavy, almost overpowering. The man in black whimpered before the altar. He tried to say *sanctuary* again, but he couldn't get his voice to work.

Another voice answered him, from the darkness beyond the church's doorway. Harsh and menacing, and yet soft and slow as bitter treacle, it sounded like several voices whispering together, in subtle harmonies that grated on the soul like fingernails drawn down a blackboard. It wasn't a human voice. It was both more and less than human.

"There is no sanctuary, here or anywhere, for such as you," it said, and the man in black trembled to hear it. "There is nowhere you can run where we cannot follow. Nowhere you can hide where we cannot find you. Give back what you have taken."

The man in black still couldn't find the courage to look back at what had finally caught up to him, but he clutched his black cloth parcel to his breast and did his best to sound defiant.

"You can't have it! It chose me! It's mine!"

There was something standing in the doorway now, something darker and deeper than the shadows. I could feel its presence, its pressure, like a great weight in the night, as though something huge and dense and utterly abhuman had found its way into the human world. It didn't belong here, but it had come anyway, because it could. The odd, whispering voice spoke again.

"Give it to us. Give it to us now. Or we will tear the soul out of your body and throw it down into the Pit, there to burn in the flames of the Inferno forever."

The face of the man in black contorted, caught in an agony of indecision. Tears forced themselves past the heavy black stitches that closed his eyes and ran jerkily down his shuddering cheeks. And, finally, he nodded, his whole body slumping forward in defeat. He seemed too tired to run any more, and too scared even to think of fighting. I didn't blame him. Even as I hid deep in my concealing shadows, that sick and pitiless voice scared the crap out of me. The man in black unwrapped his cloth parcel, slowly and reverently, to reveal a great silver chalice, studded with precious stones. It shone brilliantly in the dim light, like a piece of heaven fallen to earth.

"Take it!" the man in black said bitterly, through his tears. "Take the Grail! Just . . . don't hurt me any more. Please."

There was a long pause, as though the whole world was listening and waiting. The man in black's hands began to shake so hard he was in danger of dropping the chalice. The harmonied voice spoke again, heavy and immutable as fate.

"That is not the Grail."

A great shadow leapt forward out of the doorway, rushed down the aisle, and enveloped the man in black before he even had time to cry out. I pressed my back against the cold stone wall, praying for my shadows to hide me. There was a great roaring in the church, like all the lions in the world giving voice at once. And then the shadow retreated, seeping slowly back up the aisle, as though . . . satiated. It swept through the open doorway and was gone. I couldn't feel its presence in the night any more. I stepped cautiously forward, and studied the figure still crouching before the altar. It was now a gleaming white statue, wearing a tattered black suit. The white hands still held the rejected chalice. The frozen white face was caught in a never-ending scream of horror.

I collected all my candles, checked to make sure I'd left no traces of my presence anywhere, and left St. Jude's. I walked home slowly, taking the pretty route. I had a lot to think about. The Grail . . . if the Holy Grail had come to the Nightside, or if the usual interested parties even thought it had, we were all in a for a world of trouble. The kind of beings who would fight for possession of the Grail would give even the Nightside's toughest movers and shakers a real run for their money. A wise man would consider the implications of this, take a long holiday, and not come back till the rubble had finished settling. But if the

Grail really was here, somewhere . . . I'm John Taylor. I find things.

There just had to be a way for me to make a hell of a lot of money out of this.

Possibly literally.

TWO

The Gathering Storm

Strangefellows is the kind of bar where no-one gives a damn what your name is, and the regulars go armed. It's a good place to meet people, and an even better place to get conned, robbed, and killed. Not necessarily in that order. Pretty much everybody who is anybody, or thinks they are or should be, has paid Strangefellows a visit at one time or another. Tourists are not encouraged, and are occasionally shot at on sight. I spend a lot of time there, which says more about me than I'm comfortable admitting. I do pick up a lot of work there. I could probably justify my bar bill as a business expense. If I paid taxes.

It was still three o'clock in the morning as I descended the echoing metal staircase into the bar proper. The place seemed unusually quiet, with most of the usual suspects conspicuous by their absence. There were people, here and there, at the bar and sitting at tables, plus a whole bunch of customers who couldn't have passed for people even if I'd put a bag over my head as well as theirs . . . but no-one important. No-one who mattered. I stopped at the foot of the stairs and looked around thoughtfully. Must be something big happening somewhere. But then, this is the Nightside. There's always something big happening somewhere in the Nightside, and someone small getting shafted.

The bar's hidden speakers were pumping out King Crimson's "Red," which meant the bar's owner was feeling nostalgic again. Alex Morrisey, owner and bartender, was behind the long wooden bar as usual, pretending to polish a glass while a sour-faced customer bent his ear. Alex is a good person to talk to when you're feeling down, because he has absolutely no sympathy, or the slightest tolerance for self-pity, on the grounds that he's a full-time gloomy bugger himself. Alex could gloom for the Olympics. No matter how bad your troubles are, his are always worse. He was in his late twenties, but looked at least ten years older. He sulked a lot, brooded loudly over the general unfairness of life, and had a tendency to throw things when he got stroppy. He always wore black of some description, (because as yet no-one had invented a darker colour) including designer shades and a snazzy black beret he wore pushed well back on his head to hide a growing bald patch.

He's bound to the bar by a family geas, and hates every minute of it. As a result, wise people avoid the bar snacks.

Above and behind the bar, inside a sturdy glass case fixed firmly to the wall, was a large leather-bound Bible with a raised silver cross on the cover. A sign below the glass case read *In case of Apocalypse, break glass.* Alex believed in being prepared.

The handful of patrons bellying up to the bar were the usual mixed bunch. A smoke ghost in shades of blue and grey was inhaling the memory of a cigarette and blowing little puffs of himself into the already murky atmosphere. Two lesbian undines were drinking each other with straws, and getting giggly as the water levels rose and fell on their liquid bodies. The smoke ghost moved a little further down the bar, just in case they got too drunk and their surface tensions collapsed. One of Baron Frankenstein's more successful patchwork creations lurched up to the bar, seated itself on a barstool, then checked carefully to see whether anything had dropped off recently. The Baron was an undoubted scientific genius, but his sewing skills left a lot to be desired. Alex nodded hello and pushed across an opened can of motor oil with a curly-wurly straw sticking out of it. At the end of the bar, a werewolf was curled up on the floor on a threadbare blanket, searching his fur for fleas and occasionally licking his balls. Because he could, presumably.

Alex looked up and down the bar and sniffed disgustedly. "It was never like this on *Cheers*. I have got to get a better class of customers." He broke off as the magician's top hat on the bar beside him juddered briefly, then a hand emerged holding an empty martini glass. Alex refilled the glass from a cocktail shaker, and the hand withdrew into the hat again. Alex sighed. "One of these days we're going to have to get him out of there. Man, that rabbit was mad at him." He turned back to the musician he'd been listening to and glared at him pointedly. "You ready for another one, Leo?"

"Always." Leo Morn finished off the last of his beer and pushed the glass forward. He was a tall slender figure, who looked so insubstantial it was probably only the weight of his heavy leather jacket that kept him from drifting away. He had a long pale face under a permanent bad hair day, enlivened by bright eyes and a distinctly wolfish smile. A battered guitar case leaned against the bar beside him. He gave Alex his best ingratiating smile. "Come on, Alex, you know this place could use a good live set. The band's back together again, and we're setting up a comeback tour."

"How can you have a comeback when you've

never been anywhere? *No,* Leo. I remember the last time I let you talk me into playing here. My customers have made it very clear that they would rather projectile vomit their own intestines rather than have to listen to you again, and I don't necessarily disagree. What's the band called . . . this week? I take it you are still changing the name on a regular basis, so you can still get bookings?"

"For the moment, we're Druid Chic," Leo admitted. "It does help to have the element of surprise on our side."

"Leo, I wouldn't book you to play at a convention for the deaf." Alex glared across at the werewolf on his blanket. "And take your drummer with you. He is lowering the tone, which in this place is a real accomplishment."

Leo ostentatiously looked around, then gestured for Alex to lean closer. "You know," he said conspiratorially, "if you're looking for something new, something just that little bit special to pull in some new customers, I might be able to help you out. Would you be interested in . . . a pinch of Elvis?"

Alex looked at him suspiciously. "Tell me this has nothing at all to do with fried banana sandwiches."

"Only indirectly. Listen. A few years back, a certain group of depraved drug fiends of my acquaintance hatched a diabolical plan in search of the greatest possible high. They had tried absolutely everything, singly and in combination, and were desperate for something new. Something more potent, to scramble what few working brain cells they had left. So they went to Graceland. Elvis, as we all know, was so full of pills when he died they had to bury him in a coffin with a childproof lid. By the time he died, the man's system was saturated with every weird drug under the sun, including several he had made up specially. So my appalling friends sneaked into Graceland under cover of a heavy-duty camouflage spell, dug up Elvis's body, and replaced it with a simulacrum. Then they scampered back home with their prize. You can see where this is going, can't you? They cremated Elvis's body, collected the ashes, and smoked them. The word is, there's no high like . . . a pinch of Elvis."

Alex considered the matter for a moment. "Congratulations," he said finally. "That is the most disgusting thing I've ever heard, Leo. And there's been a lot of competition. *Get out of here. Leo. Now.*"

Leo Morn shrugged and grinned, finished his drink, and went to grab his drummer by the collar. His place at the bar was immediately taken by a new arrival, a fat middle-aged man in a crumpled suit. Slobby, sweaty, and furtive, he looked like he should have been standing in a police identification parade somewhere. He smiled widely at Alex, who didn't smile back.

"A splendid night, Alex! Indeed, a most fortunate

night! You're looking well, sir, very well. A glass of your very finest, if you please!"

Alex folded his arms across his chest. "Tate. Just when I think my day can't get any worse, you turn up. I don't suppose there's any chance of you paying your bar bill, is there?"

"You wound me, sir! You positively wound me!" Tate tried to look aggrieved. It didn't suit him. He switched to an ingratiating smile. "My impecunious days are over, Alex! As of today, I am astonishingly solvent. I . . ."

At which point he was suddenly pushed aside by a tall, cadaverous individual, in a smart tuxedo and a billowing black opera cape. His face was deathly pale, his eyes were a savage crimson, and his mouth was full of sharp teeth. He smelled of grave dirt. He pounded a corpse-pale fist on the bar and glared at Alex.

"You! Giff me blut! Fresh blut!"

Alex calmly picked up a nearby soda syphon and let the newcomer have it full in the face. He shrieked loudly as his face dissolved under the jet of water, then he suddenly disappeared, his clothes and cloak slumping to the floor. A large black bat flapped around the bar. Everyone present took the opportunity to throw things at it, until finally it flapped away up the stairs. Alex put down the syphon.

"Holy soda water," he explained, to the somewhat startled Tate. "I keep it handy for certain cocktails.

Bloody vampires . . . that's the third we've had in this week. Must be a convention on again."

"Put it from your thoughts, dear fellow," Tate said grandly. "Tonight is your lucky night. All your troubles are over. I will indeed be paying my bar bill, and more than that. Tonight, the drinks are on me!"

Everyone in the bar perked up their ears at that. They never had any trouble hearing the offer of a free drink, even with King Crimson going full blast. It wasn't something that happened very often. A crowd began to form around the grinning Tate, pleased but somewhat surprised. Frankenstein's creature pushed forward his can for a refill. Alex still hadn't uncrossed his arms.

"Absolutely no more credit for you, Tate. Let's see the colour of your money first."

Tate looked around him, taking his time, making sure he had everyone's full attention, and produced from inside his jacket a substantial wad of cash. The crowd murmured, impressed. Tate turned back to Alex.

"I have inherited a fortune, my dear boy. Taylor finally found the missing will, and I have been legally proclaimed the one and only true heir; and I am now so rich I could spit on a Rockefeller."

"Good," said Alex. He neatly plucked the wad of cash out of Tate's hand, peeled off half of it and gave the rest back. "That should just about cover your tab.

Hopefully once you've paid Taylor, he'll be able to settle up his bill too."

"Taylor?" Tate said disdainfully. He gestured grandly with what remained of his wad of cash. "I have creditors of long-standing and exhausted patience waiting to be paid. They come first. Taylor is just hired help. He can take a number, and wait."

He laughed loudly, inviting everyone else to join him. Instead, everyone went very quiet. Some actually began to back away from him. Alex leaned forward over the bar and gave Tate a hard look.

"You're planning on stiffing Taylor? Are you tired of living, Tate?"

The fat man pulled himself up to his full height, but unfortunately he didn't have far to go. He glared at Alex, his mouth pulled into a vicious pout. "Taylor doesn't scare me!"

Alex smiled coldly. "He would, if you had the sense God gave a boll weevil."

He looked past Tate, and nodded a hello. After a moment, everyone else looked round too. And that was when Tate finally turned around, and saw me standing at the foot of the stairs, from where I'd been watching and listening. I started towards the bar, and people who weren't even in my way hurried to get out of it. The crowd around Tate quickly melted away, falling back to what they hoped was a safe distance. Tate stood his ground, chin held high, trying to look unconcerned and failing miserably. I finally came to a halt right in front of him. He was sweating hard. I smiled at him, and he swallowed audibly.

"Hello, Tate," I said calmly. "Good to see you. You're looking your usual appalling self. I'm pleased to hear the inheritance is everything you thought it would be. I do so love it when a case has a happy ending. Now, you owe me money, Tate. And I really don't feel like waiting."

"You can't bully me," Tate said hoarsely. "I'm rich now. I can afford protection."

His podgy left hand went to a golden charm bracelet around his right wrist. He grabbed two of the bulky, ugly-looking charms, pulled them free, and threw them onto the floor between us. There was a brief lurch in the bar as a dimensional gateway opened between the worlds and the two charms were replaced by the two creatures they'd summoned. They stood glowering between me and Tate, two huge reptiloid figures with muscles on their muscles and great wedge-shaped heads absolutely bristling with serrated teeth. The reptiloids looked at me, and I looked at them, and then they both turned to look at Tate.

"*He*'s why you called us?" said the one on the left. "You summoned us here to take on *John bloody Taylor?* Are you *crazy*?"

"Right," said the one on the right. "We don't do lost causes."

And with that, they disappeared back to where

they'd come from. Tate tried all the other charms on his bracelet, in increasing desperation, but none of them would budge. I just stood there, looking calm and relaxed and not at all bothered, while my heart slowly returned to its usual rate. Those reptiloids really had been worryingly large . . . Sometimes it helps to have a reputation as a dangerous and extremely ruthless bastard. Tate finally gave up on the bracelet and looked, very reluctantly, back at me. I smiled at him, and he seemed very, very upset.

In the end, he gave me every piece of cash, all his credit cards, all his jewellery, including the charm bracelet, and basically everything else he had on his person. And I let him walk out of the bar alive. He was lucky I let him keep his clothes. I settled down to chat with Alex, and everyone else went back to what they were doing before, vaguely disappointed because there hadn't been any blood.

Alex poured me a large brandy. "So, John, where are you living these days?"

"In the real world," I said, deliberately vague. "I commute into the Nightside to work. It's safer."

"You're not still sleeping in your office, are you?"

"No, now I'm getting regular work here, I can afford a decent place again." I checked the money I'd taken off Tate. "In fact, it may be time for an upgrade."

"Stick to the real world," said Alex. "Now you're back on the scene again, there are a lot of people out there looking for you with bad intent in their hearts. Some of them have looked in here. You'd be surprised how much certain people are willing to pay for hard information on where you rest your head. I take their money and give them all different lies."

"I sleep more soundly in the real world," I admitted. The Harrowing are always out there, somewhere. It was why I'd stayed away from the Nightside for so long.

"Glad to be back?" said Alex.

"I don't know yet. It's good to be working again. I do my best work here. It might even be where I belong. But . . ."

"Yeah," said Alex. "But. This is the Nightside, the dark side of everyone's dreams." It was hard to tell past the sunglasses, but there was an expression on his face that in anyone else I would have said was concern. "Word is, a lot of people want you dead, John. *Lot* of people. You know . . . you're always welcome to crash here, for a while. If you need a place. Somewhere you could feel safe."

"Thanks," I said. I was touched, but knew better than to show it. It would only embarrass him. "I'll bear it in mind. So, what's new?"

Alex considered. "Surprisingly, not a lot. Jessica Sorrow, of course, but you know about that. Don't know if it's connected, but a lot of the usual players have dropped out of sight just recently. Keeping their heads down and hoping not to be noticed. Or it could be connected with the latest hot rumour, which is that angels have come to the Nightside."

I had to raise an eyebrow at that. "Angels? Really?"

"From Above and Below, apparently. No-one's reported any actual sightings as yet. Probably because no-one's too sure what to look for. It's been a long time since any angel manifested in the material worlds. Demons, yes, but they're not in the same league as the Fallen . . ."

"I encountered . . . something, at St. Jude's," I said thoughtfully. "Something very nearly as upsetting as the Unbeliever herself . . . Angels in the Nightside . . . That's got to be a Sign. Of something.

"They'd better watch their step around here," Alex said briskly. "Some of the scumbags in this locale will steal anything that isn't actually nailed down, electrified, or cursed. Wouldn't surprise me if I looked out of here one morning and found St. Michael himself propped up on bricks with his wings missing."

I looked at him thoughtfully. "You don't know much about angels, do you, Alex?"

"I do my best to steer clear of moral absolutes," said Alex. "They tend not to approve of establishments like this. And they leave lousy tips."

He didn't mention his own ancestry. He didn't have to. Alex is famously descended from Arthur Pendragon on one side, and Merlin Satanspawn on the other. Merlin himself was buried somewhere under the wine cellar. He still manifested on occasion, to lay down the law and scare the crap out of everyone. Being dead doesn't necessarily stop you being a major player in the Nightside.

"Forget all your usual notions about angels," I said patiently. "All the usual images of angels as nice guys with wings, long nighties, and a harp fixation. Angels are God's enforcers, his Will made manifest in the world of men. The spiritual equivalent of the SAS. When God wants a city destroyed, or the firstborn of a whole generation slaughtered, he sends an angel. When the Day of Judgement finally comes, and the world is brought to an end, it will be the angels who do all the dirty work. They are powerful, implacable beings. I don't even want to talk about the Fallen kind."

And then there was a voice behind me. Polite, well-spoken, and tinged with an accent I couldn't place.

"Excuse me, please. Would you be John Taylor?"

I took my time turning around, careful not to look startled, even though my heart had just missed a beat. There aren't many people capable of catching me by surprise. I pride myself on being very hard to sneak up on. In the Nightside, that's a survival skill.

Standing before me was a short, stocky type with a dark complexion, kind eyes, and jet-black hair and beard, both carefully shaped. He was wearing a long, flowing coat of a very expensive cut.

"I might be," I said. "Depends. Who might you be?"

"I am Jude."

"Hey, Jude."

He frowned slightly. It was clear he didn't get the reference. I smiled patiently.

"I'm Taylor. What can I do for you, Jude?"

He glanced at Alex, then took in the other beings lining the bar, all pretending not to listen with varying amounts of skill. Jude turned back and met my gaze steadily. "If we could talk in a private place, Mr Taylor. I have a commission for you. It pays very well."

"You just said the magic words, Jude. Step into my office."

I led him to one of the private booths at the back of the bar, and we sat down facing each other across the table. Jude gazed around the bar. It was clear this was all unknown territory to him. He didn't look like the kind of person you'd find in a bar, though on the other hand I wasn't sure where I would place him. There was something about the man . . . He didn't fit any of the usual patterns. He looked like someone with secrets. He fixed me again with those warm brown eyes, as though willing me to like him, and leaned forward across the table to address me, his voice low and confidential.

"I represent the Vatican, Mr Taylor. The Holy Father wishes you to find something for him."

"The Pope wants to hire me? What happened? Somebody steal his ring?"

"Nothing so trivial, Mr Taylor."

"Why didn't he send a priest?"

"He did. I'm . . . undercover." He glanced around the bar again, and didn't seem at all pleased or comfortable with what he saw. It wasn't so much that he looked judgemental, more . . . mystified, and perhaps even uneasy. He looked back at me and smiled almost shyly. "I don't get out much, these days. It's been a long time since I was out in the world. I was chosen to approach you because I have . . . some special knowledge of the missing item. You see, normally I'm in charge of the Forbidden Library at the Vatican. The secret, hidden chambers underground, where the Church stores texts too dangerous or too disturbing for most people."

"Like the Gospel According to Pilate?" I couldn't help showing off a little. "The translation of the Voynich Manuscript? The Testimony of Grendel Rex?"

Jude nodded slightly, giving nothing away. "Things like that, yes. I am here because an object of great power has suddenly resurfaced in the world, after being missing for centuries. And, of course, it has turned up here in the Nightside."

It was my turn to nod and look thoughtful. "This

object of power must be something really important, if the Vatican's getting personally involved. Or . . . something really dangerous. What exactly are we talking about here?"

"The Unholy Grail. The cup that Judas drank from at the Last Supper."

That stopped me in my tracks. I had to sit back in my chair and consider that for a few moments. "I never heard . . . of an Unholy Grail."

"Not many have," said Jude. "Luckily for us all. The Unholy Grail magnifies all evil by its presence, encourages and accelerates evil trends and events, and utterly corrupts all who come into contact with it. It is also a source of great power . . . It's passed from hand to hand down the centuries. Previous owners are said to include Torquemada, Rasputin, and Adolf Hitler. Though if Hitler had possessed all the mystical items rumour has gifted him with, he wouldn't have lost the war. Anyway, the Unholy Grail is currently on the loose and up for grabs, somewhere in the Nightside."

I felt like whistling loudly, impressed, but I didn't. I had a reputation to maintain. "No wonder there are angels in the Nightside."

"Already?" Jude leaned forward sharply. His eyes didn't look kind any more. "Are you sure?"

"No," I said calmly. "So far it's only talk. But the word is, we have visitors from Above and Below."

"Shit," said Jude, startling me just a bit. You don't expect language like that from a priest and librarian.

"Mr Taylor, it's imperative you locate the Unholy Grail for us, before agents of the Lord or the Enemy become directly involved. Make no mistake, if agents of the Principalities go to war here, they could level the Nightside."

"If the Unholy Grail is here, I can find it," I said, giving Jude my best confident smile. He didn't seem impressed or reassured.

"It won't be easy, Mr Taylor. Even with your famous talent. A lot of people are going to be searching for the Unholy Grail, for all manner of good and bad reasons. And in the wrong hands, its power could conceivably upset the balance between Above and Below. The Last Days could come early, and we're not nearly ready yet."

"So if the angels don't destroy the Nightside, whoever gets to the Unholy Grail first could do the job too? Wonderful. I just love working under pressure."

"But you'll take the commission?"

"I can find anything. It's what I do. That is why you came to me, isn't it?"

"You came highly recommended," said Jude. "Though for the sake of your ego, I don't think I'll say by whom. Now, the Unholy Grail was being kept in the House of Blue Lights, one of the hidden complexes deep under the Pentagon. But a guard somehow got past all the defences and protections, and smuggled it out. He couldn't hang on to it, of course, the poor fool. It had just used him to escape."

I remembered the man in black at St. Jude's, and what had happened to him. The awful voice(s) had mentioned a Grail. But I didn't say anything. I had no reason to keep things from Jude, but I still wasn't ready to trust him entirely either. I was pretty sure he was keeping things from me.

"If it's here, I can find it," I said flatly. "But I'm not so sure I should turn it over to the Vatican. Your reputation's taken a series of knocks recently. Everything from banking to the Ratlines."

"The Unholy Grail would go straight from me to the Holy Father," Jude said earnestly. "And he would ensure it would be locked away and properly contained. Until the End of Time, if necessary. If you can't trust the Pope to do the right thing, Mr. Taylor, whom can you trust?"

"Good question," I said. I wasn't convinced, and he could tell. He thought for a moment.

"We only want to preserve the status quo, Mr Taylor. Because Humanity isn't ready yet for any of the alternatives. I have been authorised to offer you a quarter of a million pounds. In cash. Fifty thousand in advance."

He placed a stuffed envelope on the table between us. I didn't touch it, though my fingers were itching to. A quarter of a bloody million?

"Danger money?"

"Quite," said Jude. "You'll get the rest when you place the Unholy Grail in my hands."

"Sounds good to me," I said. I picked up the envelope and tucked it away, giving Jude my best confident smile. "You've got yourself a deal, Jude."

And then we both looked up as three large gentlemen loomed over us. They took up positions standing as close as they could get without actually joining us in the booth. I'd heard them coming, but hadn't said anything because I didn't want Jude distracted while he was talking about money. The three gentlemen glared at us both impartially. They were the best-dressed thugs I'd seen in some time, but the attitude gave them away. They might as well have been wearing *I am a mafiosa hit man* T-shirts. They looked slick and heavy and dangerous, and each of them had a gun. All three were professionally calm, forming a semicircle to cover both me and Jude, while efficiently blocking us off from the rest of the bar. No-one could see what was happening, and we wouldn't be allowed to shout for help. Not that I had any intention of doing so. The largest of the three gunmen flashed me a humourless smile.

"Forget the pew-polisher, Taylor. From now on, you're working for us."

I considered the matter. "And if I prefer not to?"

The gunman shrugged. "You can find the Unholy Grail for us, or you can die. Right here, right now. Your choice."

I smiled nastily at him, and to his credit he didn't flinch. "Your guns aren't loaded," I said.

The three gunmen looked at each other, confused. I held up my closed hands, opened them, and let a stream of bullets fall out to clatter loudly on the table-top. They pulled the triggers on their guns, and looked very upset when nothing happened.

"I think you should leave now," I said. "Before I decide to do something similar with your internal organs."

They put away their guns and left, not quite running. I smiled apologetically at Jude. "Boys will be boys. You leave the matter with me, and I'll see what I can turn up."

"Soon, please, Mr Taylor," said Jude. He fixed me with his deep brown eyes, positively radiating sincerity and earnestness. On anyone else, it would probably have worked. "We're all running out of time."

He rose to his feet, and I got up too. "How will I find you, when I have something to report?"

"You won't," he said calmly. "I'll find you."

He walked off through the bar, not looking back. Interestingly enough, people moved to get out of his way without even seeming to notice they were doing it. There was more to Jude than met the eye. Mind you, there would have to be. The Vatican wouldn't send just anybody into the Nightside. I went back to Alex, who was refilling the hand in the top hat's glass. Frankenstein's creature was moodily tightening the stitches in his left wrist. Alex nodded to me.

"Got yourself a new client?"

"Looks like it."

"Interesting case?"

"Well, different, anyway. I think I'm going to need Suzie's help for this one."

"Ah," said Alex. "One of *those* cases."

There was a crack of thunder, a flash of lightning, a billowing of dark sulphurous smoke, and a sorcerer appeared at the bar right next to me. He wore dark purple robes and the traditional pointy hat. He was tall, dark, and imposing, with long black fingernails, a neat goatee, and piercing eyes. He gestured dramatically at me, while fixing me with a ferocious glare.

"Taylor! Find the Unholy Grail for me, or suffer an eternity of my wrath!"

While the sorcerer's attention was fixed on me, Alex calmly produced a heavy bung-starter from behind the bar. He plucked off the sorcerer's tall pointy hat and hit him over the head with the bung-starter. The sorcerer yelped once, and collapsed. Alex raised his voice.

"Lucy! Betty! Time to take out the trash!"

Lucy and Betty Coltrane, Alex's body-building bouncers, arrived and cheerfully hauled away the unconscious sorcerer. Alex glared at me.

"Unholy Grail?"

"Trust me, Alex. You really don't want to know."

He sighed. "Taylor, get out of here. You're bad for business."

THREE

Meetings in Dark Places

The long and narrow alleyway outside Strangefellows was as dark, gloomy, and filthy dirty as always. The heavy blue light from the huge moon hanging over-head gave the cobbled alley a bleak, sinister air, like the uneasy streets we walk in our dreams, and never to anywhere good. Business as usual, in the Nightside. I headed for the bright city lights at the end of the alley, picking my way carefully through the rubbish littering the way. There were severed hands everywhere, and not a few feet, all hard as ice and dusted with hoar-frost. The Little Sisters of the Immaculate Chain Saw had been busy tonight. The Christmas season must be starting early this year.

A figure appeared suddenly at the far end of the alley, standing silhouetted against the glaring neon, and I stopped dead in my tracks. For a moment my heart slammed painfully against my chest, and I forgot how to breathe. The last time I'd walked down this alley, I'd been ambushed by my enemies. The faceless horrors of the Harrowing had come for me, and I'd only escaped with the help of my old friend Razor Eddie. Of course, he'd been the one who set me up for the ambush; but that's friends for you, in the Nightside.

But this time there was only the one figure, with a distinctly female silhouette, and as she started down the dark alleyway towards me, a soft golden glow appeared around her, lighting her way. She was exceedingly blonde and pretty, and almost overpoweringly voluptuous, moving with easy grace in her own pool of light. Marilyn Monroe, in her glorious prime, in her iconic white halter dress. Not a look-alike or a double, but indisputably the real thing, wrapped in glamour, bursting with life and laughter, just like in her films. Sweet and sexy Marilyn, walking in her own spotlight.

She came to a halt before me, and smiled dazzlingly. She smelled of sex and sweat and sandalwood, of roses and rot, and though her smile was as inviting as ever, there was no matching warmth in her eyes.

"Hello, sugar," she said, in a voice like a caress. "I'm so glad I found you. I've got a message for you."

"That's nice," I said, carefully non-commital.

She laughed her famous laugh, wrinkled her nose at me, and handed me a long white envelope with the tips of her fingers. "This is for you, sweetie. Inside the envelope, there's a blank cheque! Signed by Mr. Hughes himself. He wants the Unholy Grail for his collection. All you have to do is find it for him, and you can fill in the cheque for whatever amount you like. Isn't that generous of him?"

"Pardon me for asking?" I said. "But aren't you dead?"

She laughed huskily and tossed her head. Her wavy hair moved in slow sensuous waves. Being bathed in the glow of her open sexuality was like staring into a blast furnace.

"Oh, that wasn't me. Howard looks after his friends."

"I rather thought he was dead too."

"Men that rich don't die, sugar. Not if they don't want to. They just move to another plane, for tax reasons. He's mixing with some really powerful people these days."

"People?"

"Loosely speaking."

I weighed the envelope in my hands thoughtfully. I'd never been offered a blank cheque before. I was tempted. But . . . I smiled regretfully at Marilyn.

"Sorry, dear. I already have a client. I'm spoken for."

"I'm sure Mr. Hughes can match any offer . . ."

"It isn't the money. I gave my word."

"Oh. Are you sure . . . I couldn't do anything to persuade you?"

She took a deep breath, and her breasts seemed to surge towards me. I was finding it hard to breathe again.

"I'm probably going to hate myself in the morning," I said finally, "but I have to say no. My services are for sale, but I'm not."

She pouted at me with her luscious mouth. "Everyone has their price, darling. We just haven't found yours yet."

"I'm always loyal to my client," I said. "It's all the honour I have left."

"Honour," said Marilyn, wrinkling her nose again. "See how far that gets you, in the Nightside. See you again, sugar. Boop boop de boop."

She blew me a kiss, turned elegantly on her left high heel, and strode off down the alley. Her shoes made no sound on the cobbles. She walked in glamour, still in her own spotlight, like the star she was. I watched her disappear back into the neon noir of the city streets, and only then looked down at the envelope in my hand. My first impulse was to tear it up, but wiser thoughts prevailed, and I put it carefully in my inside coat pocket. You never knew when a cheque with Howard Hughes's signature on it might come in handy.

I looked around for a dark doorway. They tended to come and go, but you could always rely on a few, this close to Strangefellows. I walked over to the nearest, kicked a few hands aside, and sat down cross-legged. No-one would disturb me here, and I had work to do. If one major player already knew I was on the trail of the Unholy Grail, then it was a safe bet everyone knew. Or at least, everyone that mattered. They'd all be looking for me, and the people they'd send wouldn't all be as pleasant and polite as Marilyn. This was the kind of treasure hunt that started serious turf wars. And the last thing I needed was the Authorities getting involved. No, I needed to get my hands on the Unholy Grail as quickly as possible, and that meant using my gift. I'm always reluctant to do that, because when I use my special talent, my mind blazes like a beacon in the darkness of the Nightside, signalling to all my enemies exactly where I am. But it's my gift that makes me what I am, that enables me to be so very good at what I do.

My gift. I can find anything, or anyone. No matter how well hidden they are.

So I sat there in the deep dark shadows, my back pressed against the wall, breathed deeply, and closed my eyes, concentrating. And opened the eye deep in my mind; my third eye, my private eye. Energies swirled within me, rough and roaring, then flowed out of me, rushing off in all directions, lighting up the night so I could See everything. The thunder of a million voices descended upon me, not all of them in any way human, and I had to struggle to focus, to narrow my vision to the one thing I was searching for. The bedlam died away, and already I could begin to sense a direction, and the beginnings of distance. And then Something reached down out of the overworld, snatched my mind right out of my body, and bore it away. There was a sensation that might have been flying or falling, as the alley and the material world disappeared. And I was somewhere else.

This time, it was my turn to stand in the spotlight. A light stabbed down from somewhere above me, brilliant and blinding, holding me in place like a bug transfixed on a pin. I felt horribly naked and exposed, as though the light showed up everything inside me, the good and the bad. All around me there was only darkness, a deep concealing darkness, and somehow I could tell it was there to protect me, because I was not worthy or strong enough to see what lay beyond my small pool of light. But I could sense that I was not alone, that to either side of me there were vast and powerful presences, two great armies assembled on an endless unseen plain. There was a feeling of restless movement, and what might have been the fluttering and flapping of wings. My mind, or more likely my soul, had been hijacked. Brought into the overworld, the boundaries of the immaterial. The overworld wasn't Heaven or Hell, but it was said you could see them both from there.

A voice spoke to me from one side, and it was a harmony of many voices, like a crowd chanting in syncopation, a choir that sang only in descants. My skin crawled at the sound of it. I'd heard such a voice before, in St. Jude's. It was a powerful, imperious voice, steeped in ancient, unanswerable authority.

"The dark chalice is loose once more, travelling in the world of mortal men. This cannot be permitted. It is too powerful a thing to be abandoned to merely human hands, and so it has been decided that we shall descend from the glory plains and walk in the material world again."

A second harmonied voice spoke from the other side, rich and complex and full of discords. "Too long has the Unholy Grail wandered at random in the world of mortal men. The sombre chalice, the great corrupter. It must be placed in the right hands and allowed to fulfill its purpose. Its time has come round at last. And so it has been decided that we shall ascend from the infernal plains and walk in the material world again."

All I could think was *Oh shit . . .*

"Tell us what you know of the Unholy Grail," said

the first voice, and the second echoed, "Tell us, tell us . . ."

"I don't really know anything yet," I said. It didn't even occur to me to lie. "I've only just started looking."

"Find it for us," said the first voice, implacable as fate, as an iceberg seeking out a ship.

"Find it for us," said the second voice, relentless as cancer, as torture.

Both their voices were very loud now, beating about me in the darkness, but I refused to allow myself to flinch or quail. Show weakness before overbearing bastards like these, and they'd walk all over me. I was scared, but I couldn't afford to show it. Both sides could destroy me in a moment, for any reason or none. But they wouldn't, as long as they thought I could be of use to them. I glared out into the dark, showing impartial contempt. Angels or devils, they both spoke with the arrogance of anyone who speaks from a position of strength. But I felt pretty sure I had a question that would reveal their true position.

"If you're so powerful," I said, "why can't you find the Unholy Grail for yourselves? I thought nothing was hidden from you, or your bosses?"

"We cannot see it," said the first voice. "Its nature hides it."

"We cannot see it," said the second voice. "Its power hides it."

"But you can See what is hidden."

"So See for us."

"I don't work for free," I said flatly. "And if either of you could compel me, you'd have done it by now. So stop trying to bully me, and make me a proper offer."

There was a long pause, and the voices said together, "What would you want?"

"Information," I said. "Tell me about my mother. My missing, mysterious mother. Tell me who and what and where she is."

"We cannot tell you that," said the first voice. "We only know what it is given to us to know, and some things are forbidden, even to us."

"We cannot tell you that," said the second voice. "We know only what is said in darkness, and some things are too awful, even for us."

"So essentially," I said, "you're really nothing more than glorified messenger boys, working on a need-to-know basis. Send me back. I've got work to do."

"You do not speak to us that way," said the first voice, its harmonies rising and falling. "Defy us, and there will be punishment."

I looked across at the other presences. "Are you going to let them get away with that? If I'm hurt or damaged, you risk losing the one person who can definitely find the Unholy Grail for you."

"Do not touch the mortal," the second voice said immediately.

"You do not speak to us that way!"

"We speak how we will! We always have!"

There was a stirring and a disturbance in the darkness, as of two great armies readying themselves for war. There were angry voices, with vicious threats and vows, and ominous intent. And it was the easiest thing in the world for me to quietly slip away from them, and drop back into my body, which waited in the doorway in the alley outside Strangefellows. It had grown cold and stiff in my brief absence, and I groaned aloud as I made myself stretch reluctant muscles and pounded my hands together to get the circulation moving again. I closed my mind down tightly, pulling all my strongest mental shields into place. You don't last long in the Nightside if you don't learn a few useful tricks to guard your mind and soul from outside attack or influence. Walk around here with an open mind, and your head will end up more crowded than the underground during rush hour.

But it did mean I wouldn't be able to use my gift again. Anytime I let down my defences long enough to See, you could bet agents from Above and Below would be waiting for a chance to grab me again. And make me an offer I wouldn't be allowed to refuse. So it looked like I was going to have to solve this case the hard way: lots of legwork, asking impertinent questions, and the occasional twisting of arms.

Which meant I was going to need Suzie Shooter even more than I'd thought.

Shotgun Suzie lived in one of the sleazier areas of the Nightside, up one of those narrow side streets that lurk furtively in the shadows of the more travelled ways. Lit starkly by glaring neon signs advertising nasty little shops and studios, offering access to all the viler and more suspect pleasures and goods, at extortionate prices, of course, it was the kind of place where even the air tastes foul. The neon flickered with almost stroboscopic intensity, and painted men and women and others who were both and neither smiled coldly from backlit windows. Somewhere music was playing, harsh and tempting, and somewhere else someone was screaming, and begging for the pain to never stop.

I walked down the centre of the street, avoiding the greasy rain-slick garbage-strewn pavements. I didn't want anyone tugging at my arm or whispering coaxingly in my ear. I was careful not to catch anyone's eye, or even glance at the shop windows. It was safer that way. I didn't want to have to hurt anyone this early in the case. Suzie's place was set right in the middle of it all, between a flaying parlour and a long pig franchise. From the outside, her section of the old tenement building looked broken-down, decayed, almost abandoned. The brickwork had been blackened by countless years of pollution and neglect, covered over with layers of peeling posters, and the occasional obscene graffiti. All the windows had been boarded up. But I knew that the single paint-peeling door had a thick core of solid steel, protected by state-of-the-art locks and defences, both high-tech and magical. Suzie took her security very seriously.

I was one of the very few people she'd ever trusted with the correct entry codes. I looked around to make sure no-one was too close, or showing too much interest, then I bent over the hidden keypad and grille. (No point in knocking or shouting; she wouldn't respond. She never did.) I punched in the right numbers, and spoke my name into the grille. I waited, and a face rose slowly up out of the door, forming its details from the splintered wood. It wasn't a human face. The eyes opened, one after another after another, and studied my face, then the ugly shape sank back into the wood again and was gone. It looked disappointed that it wasn't going to get to do something nasty to me after all. The door swung open, and I walked in. I was barely out of its way before it slammed shut very firmly behind me.

The empty hallway was lit by a single naked light bulb, hanging forlornly from the low ceiling. Someone had nailed a dead wolf to the wall with a rivet gun. The blood on the floor still looked sticky. A mouse was struggling feebly in a spider's web. Suzie never was much of a one for housekeeping. I strode down the hall and started up the rickety stairs to the next floor. The air was damp and fusty. The light was so dim it was like walking underwater. My feet sounded loudly on the bare wooden steps, which was, of course, the point.

The next floor held the only two furnished rooms in the house. Suzie had a room to sleep in, and a room to crash, and that was all that mattered to her. The bedroom door was open, and I looked in. There was a rumpled pile of blankets in the middle of the bare wooden floor, churned up like a nest. A filthy toilet stood in one corner, next to a battered minibar she'd looted from some hotel. A wardrobe and a dressing table and a shotgun rack holding a dozen different weapons. No Suzie. The room smelled ripe, heavy, female, feverish.

At least she was up. That was something.

I walked down the landing. The plastered walls were cracked, and pocked here and there with old bullet holes. Telephone numbers, hexes, and obscure mnemonic reminders had been scrawled everywhere in lipstick and eyebrow pencil, in Suzie's thick blocky handwriting. The door to the next room was closed. I pushed it open and looked in.

The blinds were drawn, as always, blocking out the lights and sounds of the street outside, and for that matter, the rest of the world as well. Suzie valued her privacy. Another naked light bulb provided the main illumination. Its pull chain was held together by a knot in the middle. Takeaway food cartons littered the bare floor, along with discarded gun magazines, empty gin bottles, and crumpled cigarette packets. Video and DVD cases were stacked in tottering piles all along one wall. Another wall held a huge, life-size poster of Diana Rigg as Mrs. Emma Peel, from the old *Avengers* TV show. Underneath the poster, Suzie had scrawled *My Idol* in what looked like dried blood.

Suzie Shooter was lying sprawled across a scuffed and faded green leather couch, a bottle of gin in one hand, a cigarette in one corner of her downturned mouth. She was watching a film on a great big fuck-off wide-screen television set. I strolled into the room, and into Suzie's line of view, giving her plenty of time to get used to my presence. There was a shotgun propped up against the couch, ready to hand, and a small pile of grenades on the floor by her feet. Suzie liked to be prepared for anyone who might just feel like dropping in unannounced. She didn't look round as I came to a halt beside the couch and looked at the film she was watching. It was a Jackie Chan fight fest; that scene towards the end of *Armour Of God* where four big busty black women in leather gang up on Jackie and kick the crap out of him. Good scene. The sound track seemed to consist entirely of screams and exaggerated blows. I glanced around me, but nothing had changed since my last visit. There was still no other furniture, just a bog standard computer set up on the floor. Suzie didn't even have a phone any more. She wasn't sociable. If anyone needed to contact her, there was e-mail, and that was it. Which she might not get round to reading for several days, if she didn't feel like it.

As always when she wasn't working, Suzie had let herself go. She was wearing a grubby Cleopatra Jones T-shirt, and a pair of jeans that had been laundered almost to the point of no return. No shoes, no make-up. From the look of her, it had been some time since her last gig. She was overweight, her belly bulging out over her jeans, her long blonde hair was a mess, and she smelled bad. Without taking her eyes off the mayhem on the screen, she took a long pull from her gin bottle, not bothering to take the cigarette out of her mouth first, then offered me the bottle. I took it away from her and put it on the floor, carefully out of her reach.

"Almost six years since I was last here, Suze," I said, just loud enough to be heard over the television. "Six years, and the old place hasn't changed a bit. Still utterly appalling, with a side order of downright disgusting. Garbage from all across the country probably comes here to die. I'll bet the only reason this building isn't overrun with rats is that you probably eat them."

"They're good with fries, and a few onions," said Suzie, not looking round.

"How can you live like this, Suze?"

"Practice. And don't call me Suze. Now sit down and shut up. You're interrupting a good bit."

"God, you're a slob, Suzie." I didn't sit down on the couch. I'd just had my coat cleaned. "Don't you ever clean up in here?"

"No. That way I know where everything is. What do you want, Taylor?"

"Well, apart from world peace, and Gillian Anderson dipped in melted chocolate, I'd like to see some evidence that you've been eating sensibly. You can't live on junk food. When was the last time you had some fresh fruit? What do you do for vitamin C?"

"Pills, mostly. Isn't science wonderful? I hate fruit."

"I seem to recall you're not too keen on vegetables either. It's a wonder to me you haven't come down with scurvy."

Suzie sniggered. "My system would self-destruct if it encountered anything that healthy. I eat soup with vegetables in. Occasionally. That sneaks them past my defences."

I kicked an empty ice cream tub out of the way and sighed heavily. "I hate to see you like this, Suzie."

"Then don't look."

"Fat and lazy and smug with it. Don't you have any ambitions?"

"To die gloriously." She took a deep drag on her cigarette and sighed luxuriously.

I sat on the arm of the couch. "I don't know why I keep coming back here, Suze."

"Because we monsters have to stick together." She

finally turned her head to look at me, unsmiling. "Who else would have us?"

I met her gaze squarely. "You deserve better than this."

"Shows how much you know. What do you want, Taylor?"

"How long have you been lounging around here? Days? Weeks?"

She shrugged. "I am currently between cases. Bottom's dropped out of the bounty-hunting business lately."

"Most people have a life apart from their work."

"I'm not most people. Just as well, really, considering most people depress me unutterably. My work is my life."

"Killing people is a life?"

"Stick to what you're good at, that's what I always say. Hell! When I do it, it's an art form. I wonder if I could get a grant . . . Shut up and watch the film, Taylor. I hate it when people talk during the good bits."

I sat with her and watched quietly for a while. As far as I knew, I was the closest thing Shotgun Suzie had to a friend. She wasn't much of a one for getting out and meeting people, unless it involved killing them later. She only really came alive when she was working. In between cases, she shut down and vegetated, waiting for her next chance to go out and do the only thing she did well, the thing she was born to do.

"I worry about you, Suzie."

"Don't."

"You need to get out of this dump and get to know people. There *are* some out there worth knowing."

"Men have been known to walk into my life, from time to time."

It was my turn to sniff loudly. "They usually leave running."

"Not my fault if they can't keep up." She shifted her weight on the couch and farted unself-consciously.

I glared at her. "They usually leave because you made them watch *Girl On A Motorcycle* one time too many."

"That film is a classic!" Suzie said automatically. "Marianne Faithful never looked better. That film is right up there with *Easy Rider* and Roger Corman's Hells Angels movies."

"Why did you shoot me, six years ago?" I didn't know I was going to ask that until I said it.

"I had paper on you," said Suzie. "Serious paper, backed by serious money."

"You knew that paper was false. The whole thing was a setup. You had to know that . . . but you shot me anyway. Why?"

"You were leaving," she said quietly. "How else could I stop you?"

"Oh, Suze . . ."

"Why do you think you were only wounded? You know I never miss. If I'd wanted you dead, you'd be dead."

"Why was it so important for you to stop me leaving?"

She finally turned to look at me. "Because you belong here. Because . . . even monsters need to feel they're not alone. Look, what do you want here, Taylor? You're interrupting a classic."

"Bruce Lee again?" I said, just to tease her. And because I knew I'd got as much honesty out of her as both of us could stand.

"Don't show your ignorance. This is Jackie Chan."

"There's a difference?"

"Blasphemer. Jackie's got some great moves, but Bruce Lee is God."

"Speaking of whom," I said casually, "I have a case I could use some help on."

Suzie sat up and gave me her full attention for the first time. "You have a case involving Bruce Lee?"

"No. God. There are angels in the Nightside."

Suzie shrugged and gave her attention back to the television screen. "About time. Maybe they'll clean the place up."

"Maybe. But there's a distinct possibility there might not be much left of the place by the time they'd finished with it. They're looking for the Unholy Grail. I've got a client who wants me to find it first. Thought you might like to help. The money really is extremely good."

Suzie produced a remote control from somewhere

underneath her and put the film on hold. Jackie froze in mid kick. Suzie looked at me. "How good?"

"I'm offering fifty thousand, out of my fee. You get twenty-five up front, and the rest when the job's done."

Suzie considered, her face impassive. "Is the job very dangerous? Will I have to kill lots of people?"

"Odds are . . . yes and yes."

She smiled. "Then I'm in."

And that was it. Suzie didn't really care about the money; she never did. She just went through the motions, so people wouldn't think they could take advantage of her. With her, it was always the job that mattered, the challenge. The only feelings of self-worth she had came from testing herself against forces that could destroy her. I took the money out of the envelope Jude had given me, peeled off half, and dropped it onto the couch beside her. She nodded, but made no move to pick it up. She didn't have a safe, or even a strongbox, on the unanswerable grounds that no-one was going to be stupid enough to steal from her. There were less painful ways to commit suicide. She turned off the television, stubbed out the last half inch of her cigarette on the leather couch, flicked it away, then fixed me with a steady stare.

"You have my full attention. Angels . . . and an Unholy Grail. Kinky. Bit out of our usual territory. Would silver work against angels?"

"Not even if you loaded it into a bazooka. You

could probably strap an angel to a backpack nuke and set it off, and he wouldn't even blink. Angels are major hard-core."

Suzie looked at me for a long moment. It was always hard to tell what she was thinking, behind the cold mask she used for a face. "You religious, Taylor?"

I shrugged. "Hard not to be, in the Nightside. If only because there are no atheists in foxholes. I'm pretty sure there is a God, a Creator. I just don't think he cares about us. I don't think we matter to him. You?"

"I used to tell people I was a lapsed agnostic," she said easily. "Now I tell them I'm a born-again heretic. I hung out with this bunch of Kali worshippers for a while, but they said I was too hard-core, the wimps. Mostly . . . I believe in guns, knives, and things that go bang. All of which we're probably going to need if we're going after the Unholy Grail. I take it there will be competition?"

"Lots and lots. So you don't have any problems, about going up against angels or devils?"

She smiled coldly. "Just give me something to aim at and leave the rest to me." She frowned thoughtfully. "There was a weapon I heard of once . . . The Speaking Gun. Created specifically to kill angels. The Collector tried to bribe me with it one time, to get into my pants . . ."

"I think we'll save that for a last resort," I said, diplomatically.

She shrugged. "So, where do we start?"

"Well, I thought we'd go and have a word with the Demon Lordz."

"Those gangsta wannabes? I have seen puppies in toilet paper commercials that were more threatening than that bunch of poseurs."

"There's more to them than meets the eye."

She sniffed. "There would have to be."

I stood up. Time to get the show on the road. "Grab what you need, and let's get moving, Suzie. Above and Below have already tried to lean on me. I'm pretty sure we're working against the clock on this one."

Suzie lurched ungracefully to her feet and stomped out of the room, heading for her bedroom. I waited patiently while she threw things about, looking for what she wanted. When she came back, she looked like Shotgun Suzie again. The grubby T-shirt and faded jeans were gone, replaced by gleaming black leather jacket, trousers and knee-high boots, generously adorned with steel chains and studs. She wore two bandoliers of bullets across her impressive chest, and the hilt of her favourite pump-action shotgun peered over her right shoulder from its holster on her back. A dozen assorted grenades hung from her belt. She'd even brushed her hair and slapped on some make-up. She looked sharp and deadly and very alive. Suzie Shooter was on the job, heading into deadly peril, and she couldn't have been any happier.

"Damn," I said. "Clark Kent becomes Superman."

"Big Boy Scout," she sneered. "Who's our client on this one, Taylor?"

"The Vatican. So watch your language. You ready?"

"Does the Pope shit in the woods? I was born ready."

I made a mental note to keep her well away from Jude, and led the way out. It was a good day for someone else to die.

FOUR

Demons, Nazis, and Other Undesirables

We went uptown. The nastiest, scariest, sleaziest joints are always uptown. Where the beautiful people go, to act out their inner ugliness in private places. Uptown, where the neon becomes more stylised and the come-ons are more subtle. Where the best food and the best wine and the best drugs, and all the very best music can be yours, for a price. Which is sometimes money and sometimes self-respect, and nearly always your soul, in the end. Uptown, you can see everybody on the way up, and everyone on the way down. Birds of a feather groom together.

Walking the rain-slick streets under hot neon, with

Suzie at my side like a barely restrained attack dog, it quickly became clear that there really were a lot fewer people about than usual. Just the thought of visiting angels, from Above or Below, had been enough to scare a lot of familiar faces into lying low for a while. But there were still crowds of people out and about, hurrying along temptation's rows, avoiding eye contact, lips wet with anticipation. On their way to business or pleasures they couldn't or wouldn't put off, even for the threat of Judgement Day.

Now and again, certain individuals would spot Suzie Shooter coming down the street towards them, and they would quickly and quietly disappear, slipping into convenient side streets and alleyways. Others would hide in doorways or deep shadows, shoulders hunched, heads down, hoping not to be noticed. A few actually stepped off the pavement and out into the road, to be sure of giving her plenty of room. A dangerous act in itself. It was never wise to get too close to any of the endless traffic that roared through the Nightside. Not everything that looked like a car was a car. And some of them were hungry.

When you go uptown, into neatly laid-out squares with tree-lined streets and ornate old-fashioned lampposts, passing increasingly expensive establishments with pretence to class and sophistication, you move among a much higher class of scumbag. There are restaurants where you have to book months in advance just to be sneered at by a waiter. Huge department stores, selling every bright and gaudy useless luxury the covetous heart could desire. Wine cellars, dispensing beverages older than civilisation that madden and inflame and bestow terrible insights. Weapon shops and influence peddlers, and quiet parlours where destinies can be adjusted and reputations restored. And, of course, all the hottest brand names and the very latest fads. Love for sale, or at least for rent, and vengeance guaranteed.

And nightclubs like you wouldn't believe.

The Nightside has the best nightclubs, hot spots, and watering holes in the world. The doors never close, the music keeps on playing, and the excitement never ends. Nowhere is the scene more now, the girls more glamorous, the setting more decadent, or the shadows more dangerous. These are places where they eat the unwary alive, but that's always been part of the attraction. The Blue Parrot, The Hanging Man, Caliban's Cavern, and Pagan Place. Once past the ominous doormen and the reinforced doors, there's every kind of music on the menu, including some live acts you would have sworn were dead. Robert Johnson, still playing the blues with weary fingers, to pay off the lien on his soul. Glenn Miller and his big band sound, still calling Pennsylvania 6-500. (The Collector had Miller on ice for a long time, but was leasing him out now, in return for a consideration best not discussed in public.) Buddy Holly, hitting his guitar like it might fight back, headlining the Rock & Roll

Sky-Diving All-Stars. And the Lizard King himself, on tour from Shadows Fall, that small town in the back of beyond where legends go to die when the world stops believing in them. Plus a whole bunch of Elvises, John Lennons, and Jimi Hendrixes, of varying authenticity. You paid your money and you took your choices.

Suzie and I were on our way to The Pit. A relatively new concern, recommended for the seriously discerning pleasure-seeker. An extremely private place, for those in whom pleasure and pain combine to form a whole far greater than the sum of its parts. Where caressing hands had sharpened fingernails, and every kiss left a little blood in the mouth. The Pit, not surprisingly, was underground. From the street up, the place was just another restaurant, specialising in meals made from extinct animals. To get to The Pit, you had to go down a long set of dirty stone steps, to an alley well below street level. No flashing neon here, no dazzling come-ons. You either knew what you were looking for, and where to find it, or you weren't the kind of patron The Pit wanted to attract. It was the kind of place where if you had to ask the price of something, you couldn't afford it. I'd been there once before, to rescue a succubus who wanted out of her contract. It all got rather messy and unpleasant, but that's life for you. In the Nightside.

Suzie and I walked down the alley, ignoring the long queue. A few of those we passed scowled and muttered, but no-one said anything. Suzie and I are well-known faces, and our reputations went before us. A few people produced camcorders, just in case there was trouble. The solid steel door that was the only entry into The Pit was guarded by two of the Demon Lordz, scowling menacingly at one and all, their muscular arms folded across their heavy chests.

At first glance, the Lordz looked like just another street gang. Both wore dark, polished leathers, fashionably scruffy, and heavy with metal studs and hanging chains. They wore bright tribal colours on their faces, gaudy daubs on skin so black it glistened blue. They wore strap-on devil's horns on their foreheads, and when they smiled or scowled they showed teeth filed to sharp points. But there was something more about them, in their unnatural stillness, in the boiling air of menace they projected, that showed they were so much more than just another set of gangsta wannabes. Certainly none of the punters waiting patiently to get in even thought about trying to jump the queue. They were mostly rich kids, in all the latest fetish gear, whose parents could probably buy and sell The Pit out of petty cash, but none of that mattered here. It wasn't who you were, but who you knew, that got you in.

Suzie studied the two Lordz standing guard before the firmly closed door and scowled ominously as they refused even to notice our presence. She tended to take such slights personally. She looked around the alley, then sneered impartially at the Lordz and the queue.

"You know all the best places to bring a girl, Taylor. I just know I'm going to have to disinfect my boots later. Do we have anything resembling a plan?"

"Oh, I thought we'd just barge our way in, insult all the right people, and kick the crap out of anyone who annoys us."

Suzie smiled briefly. "My kind of party."

I walked right up to the Lordz, radiating confidence. Suzie stuck close beside me, still scowling. Some of the queue decided that they'd try another club. The doormen finally deigned to acknowledge our existence. They were trying hard to look cool and aloof, and not quite bringing it off. The clenched fists gave it away. The one on the left looked down on me from his full six feet four.

"Back of the queue," he growled out of one corner of his mouth. "No jumping. No bribes. No exceptions. Members only. And you two would be wasting your time anyway. We have a very strict dress code."

"So piss off," said the one on the right, from his full six foot six. "Before we have to do something to you that might upset the nice ladies and gentlemen in the queue."

"Let me kill them, Taylor," said Suzie. "It's been a slow night so far."

"Keep your bitch under control, Taylor," said the one on the left. "Or we'll take her inside and teach her some manners. We might let you have her back, in a week or two, when we've broken her in properly."

Suzie's shotgun all but whistled as it flew out of the holster on her back, and the Demon Lord shut up suddenly as she rammed both barrels up his nostrils.

"I'd really like to see you try," she said, smiling her awful smile.

"This," I explained to the Demon Lordz, "Is Suzie Shooter. Also known as Shotgun Suzie, also known as Oh Christ, it's her, run."

"Oh *shit*," said both doormen, pretty much in unison. Most of the waiting queue decided at that point that it was time they were somewhere else, their hurrying feet clattered loudly down the alley. But a few actually pressed forward a little, murmuring with excitement, their eyes hot and hungry for a little real blood and death to start the evening off with a bang. The Demon Lord with the gun up his nose tried to stand even stiller than usual, while the other doorman spoke urgently into a concealed speaker grille beside the door. There was a pause, just long enough for all parties concerned to get uneasy, then the heavy steel door swung backwards, and bright light and hot and heavy music spilled out into the night air. I sauntered into The Pit, doing my best to look like I was slumming, while Suzie gave the doormen a really nasty grin before following me in, still covering both Demonz with her shotgun, until the door had closed completely between them. She started to holster her gun, then took a good look around her, and decided to hold on to it.

It was hellishly noisy inside The Pit, with death metal guitars blasting from concealed speakers. The lighting was stark and harsh and almost painfully bright. No comforting gloom here, no shadows to hide in; everything was right out in the open, so every act and reaction could be enjoyed and savoured by the milling crowd. Most of the club's patrons eddied back and forth across the open floor of the great ball-room, looking tastefully chic in gothic leathers, cut-away rubber, and spray-on latex. But the real action was taking place in spotlit nooks and crannies around the perimeter.

The bare stone walls had been decorated to look as much like a medieval dungeon as possible, and every-where you looked there were happy victims being stretched on racks, or suspended in hanging cages, or enjoying the embrace of an iron maiden, filled with hypodermic needles instead of metal spikes. There were always new shrieks of pain and joy, and howls of approval from the rapt onlookers. The victims writhed languorously as they suffered, playing to the crowd. Here and there a tall dominatrix, beautiful as a sharpened knife, all dark leathers and straps and buckles, would stride proudly through the throng in search of prey, her painted face haughty with indiffer-ence. Men and women bowed low to these mistresses of pain and tried to lick their polished boots as they passed. There were whippings and scourgings and brandings, to the delight of all concerned. Blood flowed and fell, and trickled away down hidden runnels in the floor. The close air stank of fresh sweat, cheap perfume, and industrial-strength disinfectant.

Not unlike a dentist's, really.

Suzie looked about her, entirely unimpressed, her face heavy with disinterest. "I thought the Demon Lordz were supposed to be a street gang? What are they doing running a joint like this for high-class pervs with more money than sense?"

"They're only playing at being gangstas," I said. "This . . . is their true nature coming out."

One of the dominatrixes stalked towards us, a heavy bullwhip coiled in her hands. Her black lips widened in a cruel smile. Suzie looked round and caught the dominatrix's eye. Without missing a beat, the mistress of pain changed direction and kept going, losing herself in the crowd. She knew the real thing when she saw it. I looked around me, taking my time. None of it moved me. Here, they only played at sin and damnation. I had far too much experience of the real thing to be impressed.

Over in a corner, a man was having his nipple pierced and being a real wimp about it.

I finally caught the eye of one of the female Demon Lordz, and she came through the crowd towards me. People hurried to get out of her way. She

was tall and blonde, all legs and high tits, every inch
the Aryan ideal. She wore the same scruffy outfit and
bright tribal colours as the two at the door, right down
to the fake horns on her head. She came to a halt before me, smiling coldly with blue lips to show off her
pointed teeth. Her eyes were black on black. She had
to know Suzie was covering her with the shotgun, but
she showed no signs of caring.

"What are you doing back here, Taylor? I thought
we made it very clear after your last visit that you
were never to darken our doors again."

"Just visiting," I said calmly. "Seeing how the
other five per cent lives. I love what you've done
with this place. Very atmospheric. Just the ticket, if
you want to play at being damned for a while. But
then, you'd know all about that, wouldn't you?"

"You don't belong here," said the female Demon.
"Either of you. Not your kind of scene, is it?"

Suzie sniffed loudly, entirely unmoved by the
sweaty suffering going on around her. She didn't care
much about other people's lives at the best of times.
And I knew better than to show any signs of condem-
nation or compassion. The Demon would only have
seen it as a sign of weakness. I've never had any time
for emotional excesses. I can't afford to be vulnerable, or give up any part of my self-control. Only rigid
self-discipline has kept me alive in the Nightside. It
keeps me one step ahead of the forces that have been
trying to kill me ever since I was a small child.

I felt almost wistful, watching the happy S&M freaks at their play. Must be nice to be able to *pretend* that you're in danger, while still being absolutely safe. Their various practices didn't upset or disturb me. You learn tolerance early in the Nightside. You can't keep on being outraged all the time. It wears you out.

"What do you *want,* Taylor?"

I smiled pleasantly at the female Demon. "I want to see Mr. Bones and Mr. Blood. I'm here on business. And the sooner they agree to see me, the sooner I can get my business over with, and Suzie and I can be on our way. Keep us waiting around, and we're bound to find some trouble to get into. We're already freaking out some of your customers. They came here for the illusion of danger, not the real thing."

The female Demon looked around quickly. A few of the bright young things were already drifting towards the door, shooting uneasy glances at Suzie. The blonde Demon snarled and headed for the winding metal steps that led up to the next floor. Suzie and I followed after her, sticking close as we passed through the merry throng. Someone pinched my arse. They wouldn't have dared pinch Suzie's. Out of the corners of my eyes, I could see other Demon Lordz working their way through the crowd to join us. There seemed to be quite a few of them.

The steps led up to a private office that took up the whole of the next floor. Another steel door sealed the office off from the partying below. The female Demon hammered on the door with her fist, while glaring into the lens of an overhead security camera. More Demon Lordz were climbing the steps, cutting off our retreat. Not that I had any intention of retreating until I'd got what I wanted. Suzie was looking out over the company below. Her upper lip curled briefly.

"You don't approve?" I said quietly.

"Amateur night," Suzie said dismissively. "I take pain seriously."

There were any number of ways I could have pursued that remark, but I chose not to follow any of them. Sometimes, that's what friends are for. I looked down the steps, and a dozen Demonz glared back at me. I gave them my best *I know something you don't* smile. They didn't seem particularly impressed. The door finally opened, and the female Demon led us into the private office.

The noise shut off abruptly as the door closed behind the last of the Demon Lordz. We could have been on another planet. Excellent soundproofing, though whether magical or high-tech wasn't immediately apparent. The whole floor had been converted into one very comfortable meeting place, stuffed with every kind of luxury and indulgence imaginable. Chairs so comfortable that Rip Van Winkle would never have woken up if he'd dozed off in one of them. A massive drinks cabinet, with every potable in the world, plus a few from stranger places. Winter wine, wormwood brandy, crème de Tartarus. Bowls on low tables, full of multi-coloured pills and assorted powders. A dozen large television screens covered one wall, all showing different video games. A fifteenth-century hanging tapestry, depicting the fall of Lucifer, not quite long enough to conceal the old and recent blood-stains on the carpet below it, shut off one corner. Most of the floor was glass, presumably reinforced, so that we could all look down on the mortals below, going about their various painful pleasures in eerie silence. All they saw was a mirror, showing what they loved most: themselves. Somebody cleared his throat pointedly, and I looked down the length of the office at Mr. Blood and Mr. Bones, standing on either side of their heavy mahogany desk. They ran the Demon Lordz, as well as The Pit. Neither of them looked at all happy to see me.

Unlike their fellow gang members, Mr. Blood and Mr. Bones had no time for the traditional street cred look. They both wore power suits, expertly cut and tailored. Their thick black hair was slicked back from their foreheads, and there were bright flashes of gold when they smiled to show off their pointed teeth. They looked sharp and keen and very businesslike. Yuppies from Hell. Mr. Bones was tall and slender, with wasted aesthetic features. His eyes were a pale, pale blue, and the only thing colder was his smile. Mr. Blood was large and ponderous, with red beefy features. His eyes were bright pink, like an albino's.

Both Lordz held themselves with the easy arrogance of accustomed power. Behind us, the rest of the gang had filed into the office. I counted thirty-two, half and half men and women. They lounged around in various cocky postures, trying to look hard. I ignored them, knowing that would upset them the most. Suzie still had her pump-action shotgun in her hands, pointed exactly half-way between Mr. Blood and Mr. Bones. It didn't seem to worry them too much.

"Good of you to join us," said Mr. Bones. His voice was soft and effortlessly vicious, a mere breath of air. "You were beginning to disturb the dear patrons, and we can't have that, can we?"

"Indeed not," said Mr. Blood. His voice was hearty with false cheer. "Can I interest either of you in a chilled glass of Moët & Chandon? We've just opened a bottle. A little caviar, perhaps? Or maybe something a little tastier to chew on?"

He gestured amiably with a fat hand, and the hanging tapestry drew back of its own accord, to reveal a young woman hanging in chains, slumped in the corner. She was barely out of her teens, entirely naked, and quite dead. There was a big hole in her side, from where something had been feeding on her. Stubs of broken-off ribs showed in the pale red meat, and from the dark depths of the hole, it was clear that some of her internal organs had been removed. There were tooth marks on the broken ribs. Her hair was black as night, her skin was white as snow, with not even the faintest tinge of colour in her lips or nipples. And then my heart missed a beat as the dead woman slowly raised her head and looked at me. Her body was dead, but her soul remained, trapped inside. Her eyes were focussed on me, and full of suffering. She knew what was happening to her. Her mouth moved silently.

Help me . . . help me . . .

"The suffering on offer below wasn't enough for this one," said Mr. Blood. "She insisted on the real thing. And we were only too happy to oblige her. A tasty young morsel, eh, Mr. Bones?"

"What fools these mortals be," breathed Mr. Bones. "But they do make such wonderful snacks."

Suzie stepped forward and shot the dead woman in the head. At point-blank range, both barrels together blew her whole head apart, leaving nothing behind but a great crimson-and-grey splatter of blood and brains and bone fragments on the wall behind her. The headless body kicked a few times, then was still. Suzie pumped fresh bullets into position and looked calmly at Mr. Bones and Mr. Blood.

"Some things I don't put up with."

"Quite right," I said, while the two gang leaders were still numb with shock and outrage. "You forget your place, Demon Lordz. You're not at home now. Time for us to talk seriously, I think. So drop the illusions. We're not tourists. Show us your real faces."

And in the blink of an eye, the gangsta street gang and their two yuppie leaders were gone, replaced by a whole crowd of crimson-skinned medieval demons. Eight feet tall and overpoweringly brutal, they crowded together before and around us, scarlet as sin, stinking of brimstone, with goats' horns curling up from their foreheads and cloven hooves for feet. Their male and female attributes were sarcastically exaggerated. So were their fangs and claws. Long, twitching tails hung down between their bent legs. Suzie sniffed loudly, unimpressed, and glared at me.

"You know I hate surprises. So this is why you had me carve a cross in each of my bullets and dip them in holy water."

"I believe in being prepared," I said calmly. "Allow me to introduce the real Demon Lordz. A batch of very minor demons, on the run from Hell, living among us as humans for the pleasures it affords them."

"Coffee!" said the Demonz, their snarling voices overlapping. "Ice cream! Cold showers!"

"And all the mortals we can torture," said Mr. Bones. "We can't keep them away. And they pay us to do it to them!"

"Not that we do much of the tormenting ourselves, these days," said Mr. Blood. "We find it better to delegate. All our dominatrixes are fully human. No-one understands how to inflict pain better than a trained professional human. You mortals are subtler than we could ever be . . ."

"And besides, some of us had trouble with the concept of safe words," said Mr. Bones, glaring about him.

"If you're all real demons," said Suzie, "how did you escape from Hell?"

The Demonz sniggered and elbowed each other in the ribs. Mr. Blood giggled. "Why, this is Hell, Faustus, nor are we out of it. Ah, the old jokes are still the best."

"Answer the lady," I said.

Mr. Bones shrugged. "Let's just say we're political refugees, and leave it at that. We're hiding out from those who would seek to drag us back."

"If you're trying to hide," said Suzie, "why call your place The Pit? Isn't that kinda drawing attention to yourselves?"

"No-one ever said demons were smart," I observed. "And they really are only very minor demons."

The Demon Lordz moved in a little closer, flexing their claws. The stench of brimstone was almost overpowering. I could feel my eyes smarting. I smiled kindly upon them, utterly casual.

"What do you want here, Taylor?" said Mr. Bones.

"The Unholy Grail has come to the Nightside," I said.

"We know. We don't have it," Mr. Blood said immediately.

"Never thought for a moment that you did," I said easily. "It's way out of your league. But you know people. You have contacts. You hear things, from others of your kind. So if anyone knows who's got the Unholy Grail, or is closest to getting it, it's you."

Mr. Blood shook his horned head firmly. He sat on one corner of his desk, and it groaned loudly under his weight. "We don't know, and we don't want to know. We've put a lot of effort into finding our niche and not being returned. If the dark chalice, Iscariot's Bane, really has come here, then you can bet good money that all the real movers and shakers will be out after it, like sharks tasting blood in the water."

"There are angels in the Nightside," said Mr. Bones, grimacing as though he'd tasted something bitter. "Ranks and degrees far greater than us. They are death and destruction; the will of the Highest and the Lowest made manifest in the mortal world. Nothing material can hope to stand against them."

"So we are keeping our heads down and staying very quiet on the sidelines," said Mr. Blood. "Until the Elect and the Damned have finished their business here and departed. We have no intention of being found out, and dragged back Below. Not when there are still so many subtle pleasures to be enjoyed here."

"Life is sweet," said Mr. Bones. "In this tastiest of worlds."

"The Unholy Grail is a major prize," I suggested. "You could use it to bargain for power and wealth and protection."

"You don't use the Judas Cup," said Mr. Blood. "It

uses you. It is temptation and corruption, and the seduction of fools. It gives nothing that it does not take away, and damnation follows in its wake. Even such as we are frightened of the Unholy Grail."

The Demonz stirred uneasily, as though even the mention of the dark chalice was enough to call it.

"However," said Mr. Bones, "there is a prize that we could present to the movers and shakers of the Nightside that might well win us power and wealth and protection."

"Oh yes?" I said politely. "And what might that be?"

"The heads of John Taylor and Suzie Shooter," said Mr. Bones, smiling unpleasantly. "Separated from your annoying and intrusive bodies, of course. And thus we avenge ourselves on your many slights, while winning respect from all. A plan with no drawbacks."

"Hold everything," said Mr. Blood urgently. "Can I have a word with you? Have you lost your mind? This is *John Taylor* and *Shotgun Suzie* we're talking about!"

"So?"

"So I like having my internal organs where they are, and not splattered all over the surroundings! It's rather difficult to enjoy the subtler pleasures when your passionate parts have been ripped off and stuffed where the sun don't shine! These are dangerous people!"

"We outnumber them!"

"So?"

"Sweet Lucifer, you're a wimp!" said Mr. Bones. "Don't know how you got to be a demon in the first place. Kill the mortals! Rend their bodies and eat their flesh, but make sure the heads are intact!"

"Oh shut the hell up," said Suzie Shooter.

She lifted her shotgun and shot Mr. Bones point-blank. The blessed and sanctified bullets tore his crimson face right off, revealing a dirty yellow skull. He fell backwards, screaming piteously. Mr. Blood got up off his desk in a hurry and glared at his partner, writhing in agony on the floor.

"See!"

"He'll repair himself in a minute or two," I said quietly to Suzie, as she pumped fresh ammunition into place. The Demonz were circling us slowly now, nerving themselves up to attack. "No earthly weapon can defeat a demon."

"In which case," said Suzie, tracking the nearest Demonz with her gun, "this would be a really good time for the cavalry to make an appearance. Or failing that, for you to produce one of your last-minute miracle saves."

I considered the matter thoughtfully. The Demonz were closing in. Mr. Bones sat up, holding his tattered face together with his hands, as the crimson features slowly knit themselves back together. Even Mr. Blood came out from behind his desk.

"Taylor!" said Suzie. "Anytime now would be good!"

I held up a hand and smiled. Everyone stopped moving.

"In the Beginning," I said, "God said *Let there be light,* and there was. If a man could summon up that light, from the very first moments of creation, and look into it without burning out his eyes or his reason, then that man would have at his command a light that could burn away all the darkness in the world."

For a long moment, nobody said anything. Mr. Bones stood up, glaring out of his ravaged face.

"You don't have that kind of power!"

"Don't I?" I said.

The Demonz looked at each other, remembering things I'd done and other things I was supposed to have done. I smiled at them easily.

"Just . . . get out of here," said Mr. Bones. "Get out, and leave us alone. We don't have your bloody Grail."

"Then point me at someone who might."

"Try the Fourth Reich," Mr. Blood said quietly. "They've been throwing around some serious money for information on the dark chalice. If nothing else, they'll have better information than we do."

"See how easy it can be, when everyone acts reasonable?" I said. "There's a lesson for us all in that, I feel. Time we were leaving. Don't bother to show us out."

*   *   *

We left The Pit behind us and strolled off into the night. If anything, the streets were even emptier. I knew where the Fourth Reich had their quarters. Everyone did. They publicized it hard enough, with everything from leaflets handed out in the street to prime-time advertising. The New Nazi Crusade, or the panzerpoofters, as everyone else called them, weren't short of money. Just followers. They met regularly in an old assembly room right on the edge of uptown. Monied or not, no-one wanted them any closer than that. Last I heard, they were down to a hundred members or so, and they'd given up holding uniformed parades after a dozen golems turned up at the last one to kick their nasty arses up one side of the street and down the other. But they did still have serious financial backers. They might not have the Unholy Grail themselves, but they might well have been able to buy information on who did.

Suzie looked at me suddenly. "Could you really have summoned up the light of Creation?"

I smiled. "What do you think?"

"I never know when you're bluffing."

"Neither does anyone else. That's the point."

"I notice you're not answering the question."

"Ah, Suzie, don't you want a little mystery in your life?"

She sniffed. "The only mystery in my life is why I continue to put up with you."

And that was when a figure stepped imperiously out of the shadows ahead, blocking our way. A city gent in a smart suit, complete with bowler hat and rolled umbrella, stood smiling before us. Late forties, cold eyes and colder smile, charming and sophisticated and every bit as dangerous as a coiled cobra. Suzie drew her shotgun and aimed it at him in one smooth motion.

"Relax, Suzie," said Walker. "It's only me."

"I know it's you," said Suzie.

She kept her shotgun trained on him as he approached unhurriedly. Walker, to do him credit, didn't seem in the least perturbed. It was part of his style that nothing ever touched him, despite the many fateful decisions he had to make every day. Walker represented the Authorities, the people in the background who really run things in the Nightside. Inasmuch as anybody does. Don't ask me who these shadowy people might be. I've no idea. No-one has. Sometimes I wonder if even Walker knows for sure. Still, he spoke on their behalf, and his word was law, with any amount of force available to back him up. People lived and died at Walker's word, and he'd never been known to give a damn. He came to a halt before us, leaned casually upon his umbrella and raised his bowler politely to Suzie.

"I hear you're looking for the Unholy Grail," he said. "Along with practically everyone else in the Nightside who considers himself or herself a power or a player. I, on the other hand, have been instructed by my superiors to withdraw all my people from the Nightside. The word is that I am to let the angels from Above and Below fight it out among themselves. And if anyone here gets hurt, well, if they're in the Nightside, they deserve everything that comes to them. I have the feeling the Authorities see the coming of the angels as an opportunity for a little spring cleaning. Take out the trash, so to speak. The Authorities don't care about individuals, you see. They only care about the long view, and the big picture."

"And preserving the status quo," I said.

"Exactly. Their feeling seems to be that the sooner one side or the other acquires the appalling object, the sooner they'll all leave and things around here can get back to what passes for normal. They don't like upsets like this; it's bad for business. It doesn't really matter which side ends up with the Unholy Grail; the Authorities will work out some way to turn a profit. They always do."

"This is insane," I said, keeping my voice level as my temper rose. "Don't they realise how powerful the Unholy Grail is?"

"Possibly not. Perhaps they are being overconfident. But I have my orders. Officially, none of my people can get involved. But of course, you're not one of my people, Taylor. Officially. So such restrictions don't apply to you, do they?"

I nodded slowly. "So, once again I'm doing your dirty work, am I? Cleaning up the messes you're not allowed to touch."

"It is what you do best," said Walker. "I have every confidence in you. Of course, if you screw up, you're nothing to do with me." He looked at Suzie's shotgun, still trained rock steady on him, and raised an elegant eyebrow. "My dear Suzie, as bloodthirsty as ever. You don't really think guns are going to help you against angels, do you?"

"There's always the Speaking Gun," I said, and Walker looked at me sharply.

"The depths and range of your knowledge never cease to amaze me, Taylor. But a word of warning: some cures are worse than the disease."

Suzie gave him a hard look. "You know about the Speaking Gun?"

Walker smiled coldly. "Of course, my dear. It's my job to know about things like that. I know all the weapons powerful enough to bring down or destroy the Nightside. As for the Speaking Gun, only the truly irresponsible or the seriously deluded would even consider using such a weapon."

"Any idea where such a thing might be found?" I said. "The Collector's supposed to have had it for a while."

"And couldn't hold on to it," said Walker. "Which should tell you something. Even if I did know, I wouldn't tell you. For your and everyone else's good.

Trust me on this, Taylor. You're in deep enough waters as it is."

"What is the Authorities' position on the angels themselves?" I asked, acting like I'd given up on the Speaking Gun. It didn't fool Walker in the least, but he went along with it.

"Their position is that they don't have a position. We are on the sidelines in this, and intend to stay there until all the violence and mass destruction are safely over, one way or another. Then we will return, to supervise the picking up of pieces."

"People are going to get hurt," I said. "Good people."

"This is the Nightside," said Walker. "Good people don't come here." He smiled at Suzie. "Good to see you out and working again, my dear. You know I worry about you so."

"I like to think of you being worried," said Suzie. The gun she had on him hadn't wavered once.

"Don't you care at all about the carnage that's coming?" I said, and the anger rising in my voice brought his gaze snapping back to me. "If angels go to war in the Nightside, the whole place could end up as rubble, or one big cemetery. What happens to your precious status quo then?"

Walker looked at me almost sadly. "The Nightside will survive, no matter how many people die. The major players will survive, and all the more important businesses. They're protected. No-one else matters, in the great scheme of things. And no, Taylor, I don't care how many die. Because the Nightside has never been more than a job to me. If I had my way, I'd wipe out the whole sick freak show and start over. But I have my orders."

"And the Unholy Grail?"

Walker pursed his lips, and shrugged. "I wouldn't worry too much about that. The odds are it's just another religious con job, another fake relic for fools to fight over. There have been more versions of the true Grail passing through here than there were copies of the Maltese Falcon. And even if this Unholy Grail does turn out to be the real thing, from what I've seen of its history, it's never brought anyone any real happiness or lasting power. Let the angels take it away, to Above or Below. We're better off without it. The Unholy Grail is nothing more than tinsel and glamour and shoddy dreams, just like everything else in the Nightside."

"And if it is . . . what everyone's afraid it is?" said Suzie.

"Then it's just as well you and Taylor are on the job, isn't it? So, off you go. Have fun. Try not to break anything too important. But if you do get your hands on the Unholy Grail, don't be foolish enough to hang on to the dreadful thing yourselves. I have to go to enough funerals in the line of duty as it is. The best you'll be able to achieve in this appalling business is to decide which side to hand it over to. Which may not be as straight forward as you think. You see, I know who your client really is. And you only think you do."

I started to say something, but Walker had already turned his back on us and was walking unhurriedly away. Head held high and back ramrod straight, as always. He'd said everything he'd come to say, sowed all the right doubts, and now wild horses couldn't drag another word out of him. I shook my head slowly. No-one can mess with your mind like Walker.

Suzie continued to cover him with her shotgun until he rounded a corner and was safely out of sight, then she holstered the gun with one swift motion, and turned to me. "What was that all about, Taylor? Who is our client?"

"The Vatican, supposedly." I scowled thoughtfully. "Represented by an undercover priest called Jude."

"Like in St. Jude's?"

"Presumably. It occurs to me now that I never did check out his credentials properly. I don't usually slip up like that. There's just something about the man . . . that makes you want to trust him. Which in the Nightside should be automatic grounds for suspicion. If we do get our hands on the Unholy Grail, I think I'll make a point of asking some really awkward and pointed questions before I hand it over to anyone. Come on, Suzie. Let's get over to the Fourth Reich's headquarters. Before someone else does."

*　　*　　*

The old assembly room currently hosting the last great hope of the Fourth Reich was situated at the end of a quiet side street, in a largely residential area. The kind of place where people kept to themselves, minded their own business, and watched the world from behind drawn curtains. The street was empty, the night unusually quiet. Suzie and I strolled down the deserted street, our footsteps sounding unusually loud and carrying. No-one appeared to challenge us as we approached the assembly room. Which was also not usual. Suzie and I stopped outside the front door. It was standing slightly ajar. Suzie unholstered her shotgun, and scowled at the door. I looked at her enquiringly.

"What is it, Suze?"

"Don't call me that. It's too quiet. Those Nazi freaks always have their martial music running full blast, so they can puff out their chests and march up and down to it and shout *Heil!* at each other. This is their usual meeting time, but I can't hear a damned thing." She stepped cautiously forward and put her face to the crack of the door. She sniffed a few times. "Cordite. Smoke. Someone's been firing guns in there."

She looked at me, and I nodded. Suzie kicked the door in and charged on in, gun at the ready. I followed after her, at a more sedate pace. I don't carry a gun. I've never felt the need. I soon caught up with Suzie. She'd stopped not far inside. We stood together and looked around the old assembly room, taking our time. There was no need to hurry any more.

The long hall the Fourth Reich used as their headquarters and meeting place was a fair size. Far too big for the small-scale rallies that were all they could manage these days. And every inch of the great open floor was covered with dead bodies. Dozens of dead Nazis, all in full uniform, all of them soaked in blood and riddled with bullet holes. They lay where they had fallen, outstretched hands reaching out for help that never came, like so many discarded toy soldiers. The walls had taken a lot of hits too. The swastikaed flags and Nazi memorabilia and old curling photos covering the walls had been torn apart by sustained gun-fire. Most hung in tatters, pitiful remnants of a dead empire. And there was blood everywhere, splashed and splattered across the walls, running down to form thick pools between the bodies on the floor.

Suzie was on full alert, raking every inch of the hall with savage eyes, swivelling her shotgun back and forth, searching for an enemy or a target. Suzie only ever really came alive when there was a chance of killing someone. But there was nothing moving in the assembly room but us. The Fourth Reich was over before it even got started. This was a place of the dead now.

"Whatever happened here, we missed it," said Suzie.

"Someone else looking for the Unholy Grail got here first," I said, stepping carefully forward, over and around the piled-together bodies. "And whatever questions they asked, they sure as hell didn't like the answers they got."

"Whoever that someone was, they had a hell of a lot of firepower," said Suzie, moving cautiously forward after me. "You couldn't do this much damage with handguns. We're talking heavy-duty weaponry. Given the fire patterns, at least a dozen automatic weapons, maybe more. If the Nazis had any weapons, it doesn't look like they got the chance to use them. I don't see anyone dead not wearing a uniform." She knelt beside one corpse and checked for a pulse in the neck. She shook her head briefly and stood up. "Still warm, though. This all happened fairly recently."

I looked around me, estimating the numbers. "We're looking at . . . at least a hundred dead people here. Most of their organisation. Maybe all of it."

Suzie sniggered suddenly. "Hey, Taylor, what do you call a hundred dead Nazis? A good start."

"Cheap, Suzie, even for you. You'll be doing knock-knock jokes next." I stopped and looked at a huge poster of Adolf Hitler on the wall beside me. Blood had splashed across half his face. Some symbols are just too obvious, even for me. "They say he owned the Holy Grail."

"Didn't do the silly bugger a lot of good in the long run, did it?"

"Good point." I looked back at the dead Nazis, trying to summon up some sympathy, and failing. Given a chance, they would have done this to the whole world, and laughed while they did it. To hell with them. A thought struck me. "Men with guns did this, Suzie. Not angels."

Suzie nodded. "Hard to visualise an angel with an Uzi. What do we do now?"

"We search the place thoroughly. Just in case whoever did this missed something. Something that might tell us where to go next. I'm a private detective, remember? Find me some nice juicy clues, so I can smile enigmatically over them."

It took us the best part of an hour, but eventually we found our clue. He was kneeling behind a piano at the far end of the hall, next to a half-open fire exit door. A white statue of a man, dressed in a smart black suit. He was crouched down right next to the piano, as though trying to hide from something. And given the horrified scream still fixed on his gleaming white face, a pretty damned awful something at that. Suzie and I studied him carefully.

"Just when you think you've seen everything," Suzie said finally. "Marble?"

"I don't think so." I touched a fingertip to the contorted white face, brought the fingertip to my mouth, and tasted it.

"Well?" said Suzie.

"Salt," I said. "It's salt."

"A statue made of salt?"

"This isn't a statue. I've seen this work before, at St. Jude's. Someone, or more properly something, turned a living human being into salt, just like this."

Suzie curled her upper lip. "Kinky. Why salt?"

"Lot's wife looked back to see the Lord's angels at work. And was turned to salt."

"Creepy," said Suzie. "Big-time creepy. But why just this man, and not any of the others?"

I considered the matter. "This isn't one of the Nazis. He isn't wearing a uniform. More likely, this was one of the people who wiped out the Nazis. Because they couldn't, or wouldn't, deliver the Unholy Grail to their attackers. Then . . . the angels turned up. The ambushers disappeared out this fire exit at speed, but this poor bastard either didn't move fast enough, or thought he could hide here. Search his pockets, Suzie."

She looked at me. "Why do I have to do it?"

"Hey, I tasted his face."

Suzie sniffed, put away her gun, and frisked the statue's clothing with practiced thoroughness. A small pile of all the usual junk formed on the floor before him, while I studied the silently screaming face.

"You know, Suzie, there's something familiar about this guy."

"Nothing in the coat pockets."

"I've seen him before somewhere . . ."

"Nothing in the trouser pockets . . . except a piece

of old gum in his handkerchief. Now that is really disgusting."

"Got it!" I said triumphantly. "This guy braced me in Strangefellows, earlier tonight. He wanted me to work for his boss and didn't take it at all well when I declined."

"Who was he working for?" said Suzie, straightening up and rubbing her hands briskly against her jacket.

"He didn't say. But he knew my client was a priest, even though Jude was travelling incognito. Called him a 'pew-polisher.' Which means this guy has to be working for one of the major players. Someone with real information as to what's going on in the Nightside."

Suzie frowned. "Walker?"

"No. This isn't his style. Too crude. Besides, he said he'd taken all his people out, and I believe him. No, this has to be the work of some of the real movers and shakers. The Collector, Nasty Jack Starlight, the Smoke Ghosts, the Lord of Tears . . ."

And then my eye fell on something on the floor, tucked under the statue's ankle. A small black case, almost hidden in the shadows. I gestured to Suzie, and she helped me manhandle the salt statue to one side. It felt eerily light and strangely delicate, as though it might shatter and fall apart under rough handling. I pushed the black case out into the light with the tip of my shoe. It was about a foot long, eight inches wide, and its surface was a strangely dull matte black. Suzie prodded it with the barrel of her gun. Nothing happened. We both knelt down to study the case more closely. Neither of us felt like rushing things. We both had extensive experience of booby-traps. It took me a while to make it out, but I finally recognised a familiar symbol, set out in bas-relief on the case's lid. A large initial C, containing a stylised crown.

"The Collector," said Suzie. "I'd know his mark anywhere."

"Whatever's in the case must be important," I said slowly. "This guy stopped here to try and open the case, and the angel got him."

"A weapon?" said Suzie.

"Seems likely. But he never got a chance to use it."

"Do we open it?" said Suzie.

"Give me a minute," I said.

I couldn't afford to open my gift for finding things all the way, not with angels hovering in the over-world, waiting for the chance to grab me again. But I could ease my third eye, my private eye, open just a crack, just enough to find out what defences the Collector had built into the case. I braced myself, ready to shut down all of the way if I even sensed anyone watching me, but it only took me a few seconds to sense there were no defences, and no booby-traps. Faced with an angel, this guy must have revoked all the case's protections to try and get at the contents faster. I shut down my third eye, and re-established all my mental shields.

And then I opened the case.

The smell hit me first. The smell of hardworking horses, the scent of dogs maddened on heat, the stench of freshly spilled guts. I pushed the lid all the way back. And there, nestled in a bed of black velvet, was the ugliest handgun I have ever seen. It was made of meat. Of flesh and bone, dark-veined gristle, and shards of cartilage, held together with strips of pale skin. Living tissues, shaped into a killing tool. Thin slabs of bone made up the handle, surrounded by freckled skin. The flushed skin had a hot and sweaty look. The trigger was a long canine tooth, and the red meat of the barrel glistened wetly.

"Is that . . . what I think it is?" said Suzie.

I swallowed hard. "It fits the description." We were both speaking very quietly.

"The Speaking Gun. The Collector had it after all."

"Yes."

"Is it . . . alive, do you think?"

"Good question. No, don't touch it. You might wake it."

Suzie leaned in close, wrinkling her nose at the smell, then frowned and turned her head to one side. Strands of her long blonde hair fell down, almost touching the thing as she listened. She straightened up again and looked at me. "I think it's breathing."

"The Speaking Gun," I said. "A gun created specifi-

cally to kill angels, from Above and Below. Damn . . .
We are in deep spiritual waters here, Suzie."

"Who made it?" she said suddenly. "Who'd want
to be able to kill angels?"

"No-one knows for sure. Merlin's name has been
bandied about, but he gets blamed for a lot of
stuff . . . There's always The Lamentation or The En-
gineer, but they usually deal in more abstract
threats . . ." Something on the bone handle caught my
eye, and I leaned forward. Etched deep into the bone
were lines of tiny writing. I struggled with it for a
while, then admitted defeat. "Suzie, you take a look at
this. You've got better eyes than me."

She leaned in close again, holding her long hair
back, and slowly read out the words on the bone handle. "Abraxus Artificers. The old firm. Solving problems since the Beginning." She straightened up again,
frowned, and looked at me. "Any of that mean anything to you?"

"Not much."

"So, are we going to take it with us?"

I snorted. "I'm certainly not leaving something this
powerful lying around here. It'll be safer with us."

"Great!" said Suzie. "A whole new kind of gun for
me to use!"

"Hold everything, Suzie. I'm not sure we can afford to use a weapon like this. We kill an angel, even
a Fallen one, and you can bet *Someone* is going to get
really mad at us."

Suzie shrugged. "It's got to beat getting turned into salt."

"There is that, yes." I carefully closed the lid on the Speaking Gun, picked the case up, and slipped it carefully into my coat pocket, next to my heart. "Still, I think we should consider using this only as a very last resort."

Suzie pouted, but didn't object. "Any idea how it's supposed to work?"

"Only roughly. According to the Voynich Manuscript, the Speaking Gun re-creates God's Word. You know, in the Beginning was the Word? The great Sound at the start of Creation, that lives on in the real, secret, names of everything. The Speaking Gun recognises the secret name of whatever you point it at, and then Says it backwards, uncreating it. Theoretically, this Gun could destroy anything. Or everything."

"*Cool . . .*" said Suzie.

"The Gun is also supposed to exert a very heavy price on whoever uses it," I said sternly. "No-one today knows what. But given the fact that no-one's dared use the awful thing in centuries, I think we should be extremely cautious."

"All right," said Suzie. "No need to look at me like that. I can take a hint. I can be cautious, when I have to be. So, where do we go now?"

"Well, given that the lid of this case bears the Collector's mark, I think it's fair to assume this guy and his friends worked for the Collector. Which makes sense. He'd sell what's left of his scavenging soul to get his hands on a unique item like the Unholy Grail. He'd certainly sell any number of other people's souls for it. And you can bet good money he'll have the very latest information on where it might be. If he doesn't already have it . . . So I think we should pay him a little visit."

"Good idea," said Suzie. "Except nobody knows where to find him."

"There is that problem, yes. The location of his secret hideout is one of the great mysteries of the Nightside. Not too surprising, really. If people knew where he kept his legendary collection, they'd be lining up a dozen deep to burgle and loot it. But someone must know. This guy would have had some way of reporting back to the Collector, but his associates are long gone. So, who else do we know that works for him?"

"The Bedlam Boys!" said Suzie.

"Of course . . . They wouldn't normally betray the Collector's confidence, not even to hard cases like us, but now we have something to bargain with. He's bound to want the Speaking Gun back."

"And we'll only agree to hand it over in person."

"Got it in one. Let's go."

The Bedlam Boys, nasty little bastards that they were, often did work for the Collector. They specialised in running protection rackets, using their appalling abilities to extract regular payments from small businesses and the like. They were also very good at recovering debts. The Collector used them to persuade reluctant owners to hand over some special item that he had his eye on. Few people had the strength of will to stand against the Bedlam Boys. It shouldn't be too difficult to track them down; they made enough noise and commotion when they were working.

The black case lay snugly in my coat pocket as Suzie and I left the assembly room. It pressed heavily against my side, almost painfully hot. Suzie was right. It was breathing.

Outside the hall of the dead, in the deserted street, we stopped and looked up. The great moon hung heavily in the sky, full and bright and a dozen times larger than it seemed outside the Nightside. Things were flying across the night sky, silhouetted against the pallid face of the moon. Dark shapes, vaguely human, with huge wingspans. As Suzie and I watched, more of the things flew past, crowding together in ever greater numbers until there were hundreds of them, darkening the night, blocking out the light of the moon and the stars.

Angels had come to the Nightside. Armies of angels.

FIVE

Angels, Bedlam Boys, and Nasty Jack Starlight

There were angels all over the Nightside, crossing the night sky in such numbers that they blocked out the stars in places. At first, people came crowding out onto the streets, laughing and pointing, marvelling and loudly blaspheming, and more often than not discussing ways to profit from the new situation. And then the angels started dropping down into the Nightside like birds of prey, winged Furies in search of information and retribution, and God and the devil help anyone who dared refuse them. People were snatched up into the boiling skies, and after a time dropped screaming back into the city streets. Sometimes, only blood or body parts fell back. And sometimes, worse and stranger things were returned that were no longer in any way human. Angels are creatures of purpose and intent only, and know nothing of mercy. Soon anyone with a grain of common sense had disappeared from the streets. Suzie and I walked alone down deserted ways, and from all around came the sound of doors being locked and bolted, and even barricaded.

Like that was going to help.

"So," Suzie said, after a while, "when are you going to use your gift, to find out where the Bedlam Boys are practicing their appalling trade these days?"

"I'm not," I said shortly. "The last time I tried to use my gift, the angels ripped me right out of my head and hauled me up into the shimmering realms to interrogate me. I was lucky to get away with my thoughts intact, and I daren't risk it again. We're going to have to solve this case the old-fashioned way."

Suzie brightened up a little. "You mean kicking in doors, asking loud and pointed questions, threatening life and property, and maybe just a touch of senseless violence?"

"I was thinking more of gathering clues, piecing together information, and developing useful theories. Though there's a lot to be said for your way too."

I took my mobile out of my coat pocket and called my secretary. Actually, she's my secretary, receptionist, junior partner, and general dogsbody of all trades. I acquired Cathy Barrett on an earlier case, when I rescued her from a house that tried to eat her. I took her in, gave her a bowl of milk, and now I can't get rid of her. To be fair, she runs my office in the Nightside far more efficiently than I ever could. She understands things like filing, and keeping an appointment diary, and paying bills on time. I've never had the knack for being organised. I think it's a genetic thing. In the few months she's been working for me, Cathy's made herself indispensable, though God forbid she should ever find that out. She's insufferable enough as it is, and besides, I'd have to pay her more.

"Cathy! This is John. Your boss, John. I need some information on the current whereabouts of the Bedlam Boys. What have you got?"

"Give me a minute to check, oh mighty lord and master, and I'll see what I can dig out of the computer. Seems to me I heard something about them the other day. Do I take it it's their turn for a good kicking? Oh happy day." Cathy sounded bright and cheerful, but then she always did. I think she just did it to annoy me. "Okay, boss, got them. Seems they're running the old protection racket again, down on Brewer Street. In fact, the computer's getting updates from the crystal ball that they're shaking down the Hot N Spicy franchise on Brewer Street right now. If you hurry, you should get there before they leave. If the blonde one's there, feel free to give him a good slap on my account."

Part of Cathy's duties, when she's not working tirelessly to keep my business solvent in spite of me, is to keep track of all the major players in the Nightside, where they are, and who they're doing this week. Information is currency, and forewarned is definitely forearmed. Cathy makes a lot of contacts through her incessant clubbing, and her cheerful willingness to chat, drink, and dance with anyone still warm and breathing. It helps that she can chat, dance, and drink under the table pretty much anyone who isn't actually already dead and pickled. Cathy seems to regard alcohol as a food group, and has the endless energy of every teenager. It also helps that she's sweet and pretty and charming, and people like to talk to her. They tell her things they'd never tell anyone else, and Cathy feeds it all into the computer.

There was a time I'd have been doing the rounds myself, but I just don't have the energy any more to drink and debauch till dawn. Especially since dawn doesn't ever happen. It's always night in the Nightside. Luckily, Cathy seems to positively thrive on a regular diet of booze, caffeine, and adrenaline, and is on a first-name basis with practically every doorman and bouncer in the Nightside. You'd be surprised what people will say in front of them, not even noticing they're there because, after all, they're only servants.

I do keep up my own circle of contacts, of course. Old friends and enemies. You'd be surprised how often they turn out to be the same person, as the years go by. Some movers, some shakers, and a few that most people don't even suspect are major players. There aren't many doors that are closed to me. People tell me things. Mostly because they're afraid not to. And it all goes into the computer, too.

Between us, Cathy and I keep tabs on most things and people that matter. Cathy updates every day, and is always busy trying to spot upcoming trends and significant connections. Though we nearly lost everything last month, when the mainframe got possessed by Sumerian demons, and we had to call in a tech-nodruid to exorcise it. I'd never heard language like that before, and even after it was all over, the office still smelled of burning mistletoe for weeks.

And I might add that the computer Helpline people were no bloody use at all.

"I'm getting mass reports of angel sightings," said Cathy. "Wings and blood everywhere, and several manifestation of statues weeping, bleeding, and soiling themselves. Either the Pholio Brothers are pushing a really potent brand of weed this week, or the Nightside's being invaded. This got anything to do with you, John?"

"Only indirectly."

"Angels in the Nightside . . . that is so cool! Hey, do you think you could get me a feather from one of their wings? I've got this new hat that could look absolutely killer with just the right feather . . ."

"You want me to sneak up on an angel and rip out its pinfeathers, so you can make a fashion statement? Oh right, like that's going to happen. *No,* Cathy. Stay away from the angels, as a personal favour to me. Concentrate on the Bedlam Boys. Is there any particular reason why I should be annoyed with the blonde one?"

"He tried to chat me up last week at the Dancin' Fool," said Cathy. "Thought he could impress me because he and his brothers used to be this big boy band. As if! That is so nineties . . . Anyway, he wouldn't take *No, Get lost* or *Fuck off and die!* for an answer, so I ended up smacking him right in the eye. I swear, he was so surprised he hit top C above A. Then he started crying, so I got all guilty and danced with him anyway. And I have to say his moves were complete rubbish without his old choreographer on hand to help him out. Then he pulled me in close for a slow dance, and stuck his tongue in my ear, so I rammed the heel of my stiletto through his foot and left him to it. Wanker." She paused.

"Ooh, ooh! I just remembered! I have messages for you . . . Yes. The Pit's management called to say you and Suzie are banned. Forever. And, they may sue for emotional distress and/or post-traumatic stress disorder. And Big Nina called to say Not to worry, it wasn't crabs after all. It was lobsters."

I hung up. Some conversations, you know they're not going to go anywhere you want.

It didn't take us long to get to the Hot N Spicy franchise on Brewer Street. We could hear the trouble half-way up the street. Screams and shouts and the sounds of things breaking; all the usual signs of the Bedlam Boys at their work. People were expressing a polite interest, but from a very safe distance. The Boys' powers tend to leak out in all directions once they get started. Suzie and I threaded our way through the crowd and cautiously approached the franchise's open door. We looked in. Nobody noticed us. Everyone had problems of their own.

It was a cheap place, all ugly wallpaper and over-bright lighting and plastic tablecloths. Plastic so that they could be wiped down between customers. You can wipe pretty much anything off plastic. The Hot N Spicy franchise specialises in fire alarm chillies, all variations, one mouthful of which could melt all your fillings and set fire to your hair. Chillies from hell. Three toilets, no waiting, and they keep the loo rolls in the fridge. We are talking *atomic* chillies, and I don't want to even think about the fallout. For *real* chilli fans only. A sign on the wall just inside the door proudly proclaimed Today's Special, wasabe chilli. Wasabe is a really fierce Japanese green mustard, which ought by right to be banned under the Geneva Convention for being more dangerous than napalm.

There was another sign below that, saying *Free sushi; you supply the fish.* Enterprise is a wonderful thing.

Suzie and I eased ourselves through the open door and watched the Bedlam Boys practicing their particularly unpleasant version of the protection racket. Though consumer terrorism would probably be a better description. Once upon a time, the Boys really had been a successful boy band, but it had been a long time since any of their saccharine cover versions had even come close to troubling the charts. On the scrap heap while barely into their twenties, the Boys had drifted into the Nightside in search of a new direction, and the Collector had supplied them with a useful psychic gift in return for their talent, which he apparently keeps in a jar. A very small jar. These days, the Bedlam Boys mostly worked as muscle for hire or frighteners. And when business is slow they pick up pin money by freelancing. Either you agreed to pay them regular insurance payments, or they guaranteed bad things would happen to your business. To be exact, they turned up on your doorstep and demonstrated their awful ability on whoever happened to be present. The Boys could psionically inflict all kinds of different phobias and manias on anyone in their immediate proximity. They were currently hitting the Hot N Spicy's staff and customers with every kind of fear and anxiety they could think of, grinning widely all the while.

The place was full of screaming and crying people, staggering helplessly between overturned tables, blind to everything but the horrors that had been thrust into their minds. Staff and customers alike clutched at their heads, lashed about them with trembling arms, and pleaded pitifully for help. Some lay on the floor, crying hopelessly, thrashing like epileptics. And in the middle of all this horror and chaos, the Bedlam Boys, standing tall, looking proudly about them, and sniggering and giggling and elbowing each other in the ribs as they thrust people into Hell.

There were four of them, so alike they might have been mass-produced, with perfect bubble gum pink skin, perfect flashing white teeth, and immaculately styled hair. Hair colour seemed to be the only way to tell them apart. They all wore spangled white jumpsuits, cut away in the front to show plenty of hairy chest. They looked almost glamorous, until you looked closely at their faces. Each had the look of a dissipated Adonis, their once handsome features now marked with lines of cruelty and indulgence, like the fallen idols they were.

The franchise had become Panic Attack Central. People howled and screeched and sobbed bitterly as they were suddenly and irrationally afraid of spiders, of falling, of the walls closing in, of open spaces or enclosed places. If they could only have gathered their thoughts for a moment, they would have known these fears weren't real, but the hysteria that filled their heads left no room for rational thought. There was only the fear, and the horror, and no escape anywhere. Some of the franchise's staff and customers were made terrified of really obscure things. The Boys liked to show off. And so there was the fear of genitals shrinking and disappearing, the fear of people suddenly speaking in French accents, the fear of people showing you their holiday photos, and the fear of not being able to find your jacket.

Some of that was almost funny, until I saw one customer digging long bloody furrows in his bare arms with his fingernails, as he tried to scrape away all the bugs he felt were crawling all over him. Another man tore out his eyes with clawed fingers, and threw them on the floor and stamped on them, rather than see what he was being made to see. On the floor, people writhed and cried out in the grip of strokes and heart attacks and convulsions. The Bedlam Boys looked upon their work, and laughed and laughed.

"This is too much, even for me," Suzie said flatly. "Give me the Speaking Gun, Taylor."

"Hell no," I said immediately. "Save that for the angels. It's too big, too dangerous to risk using on anything else. Don't be impatient, Suzie. I know you're eager to try the thing out, but it didn't come with a user's manual. We have no idea of the side effects or drawbacks."

"What's there to know? It's a gun. Point and shoot."

"*No,* Suzie. We don't need the Speaking Gun to deal with cheap punks like these."

"Then what do you suggest?" said Suzie, with heavy patience. "I can't open fire with my shotgun from here. Too many innocent parties in the way. And we can't risk getting any closer, or the Boys' power will affect us too."

"What do you have a fear of, apart from tidying up? They can't affect us, as long as we shield our minds against them."

She looked at me dubiously. "Are you sure about that?"

"Actually, no. But that's what I was told. And we can't just stand here and do nothing."

But even as we stood there debating the point, one of the Bedlam Boys looked round and spotted us. He cried out, and all four Boys turned their power on us, reaching out to the very edge of their range. Their spell fell upon us, and fear stabbed into my brain like so many shards of broken glass. Concentration and willpower did me no good at all.

I was alone, standing in the ruins of London, in the Nightside of the future. I'd been here before, seen this before, courtesy of a Timeslip. A future that might be, of death and destruction, and all of it supposedly my fault. For as far as I could see in the dim purple twilight, I was surrounded by tumbled buildings and seas of rubble. There was no moon in the almost starless sky, and the still air was bitterly cold. And somewhere, hidden in the deepest, darkest shadows, something was watching me. I could feel its presence, huge and awful, potent and powerful, drawing steadily closer. It was coming for me, with blood and worse on its breath. I wanted to run, but there was nowhere left to go, nowhere left to hide. It was close now. So close I could hear its eager breathing. It was coming for me, to take me away from everything I knew and cared for, and make me its own at last. The terrible shadow that loomed over everything I did, that had dominated my life ever since I was born. Close now, vast and powerful. A great dark shape, threatening to unmake everything I'd so painstakingly made of myself.

I knew what it was. I knew its name. And that knowledge frightened me more than anything else. That finally she was coming for me, after pursuing me my whole damned life. It was almost a relief to say her name.

Mother . . . I whispered.

And in naming my fear, that unknown creature who had birthed and then abandoned me, I was suddenly so full of rage it was the easiest thing in the world to push back the fear, and deny it. My mental shields slammed back into place, one by one, and the dead world around me shuddered, becoming flat and grey and unconvincing. I pushed the Bedlam Boys out of my mind with almost contemptuous ease, and in the blink of an eye I was back in the Hot N Spicy franchise again.

I'd fallen to my knees on the grimy floor, my whole body shaking with the strain of what I'd been put through. Suzie was kneeling beside me, tears running jerkily down her face from wide, unseeing eyes, lost inside herself. I put a hand on her shoulder, and in that moment I saw what she saw.

Suzie was lying in bed in a hospital ward, held in place by heavy restraining straps. Her throat was raw from screaming. She lunged against the leather straps, but they were far stronger than her. So all she could do was lie there and watch helplessly as her fear crawled slowly, laboriously, across the ward floor towards her. It was small and weak, but determination kept it moving. It was soft and scarlet and barely formed, and it left a scuffed bloody trail behind it as it crawled slowly towards her. It was almost at the side of her bed when it painfully raised its oversized head and looked at her.

And called her *Mommy* . . .

It took all my strength to wrap my mental shields

around Suzie too, and drag her out of there and back into the waking world. She pulled away from me immediately, kneeling alone, hugging herself tightly as though afraid she might fly apart. Her face was a snarling mask of outrage and horror, tears still dripping off her chin. It was actually shocking to see her so vulnerable, so hurt. I hadn't thought there was anything that could hurt Shotgun Suzie. I started to reach out to her; then her puffed-up eyes fell upon the Bedlam Boys, and she reached for the shotgun holstered on her back. The Boys gaped at us, amazed that we'd been able to break free from their power. I fired up the dark side of my gift. For a moment, anything could have happened.

And that was when the angel arrived.

A vivid, overwhelming presence suddenly filled the restaurant, slapping up against the walls and suppressing everything else. The Bedlam Boys' power snapped off in an instant, blown out like four tiny candles in a hurricane. They just stood there and blinked stupidly at the angel. At first, it looked like a grey man in a grey suit, so average-looking in every way as to seem almost generic. You couldn't quite look at him, only glimpse him out of the corner of your eyes. And then he grew more and more real, more and more solid, more *there,* until you couldn't look at anything else. The angel lifted his grey head and looked at the Boys, and suddenly erupted into a pillar of fire in human form. His light was blinding, dazzling, too bright to look at directly. Vast glowing wings spread out behind him, sparking and spitting. There was a stench of ozone and burning feathers. The Bedlam Boys stared into the heart of that terrible light, mesmerised.

And turned to salt.

One moment they were living and breathing people, and the next there were four salt statues, paler than death, still wearing their stupid spangled jumpsuits. And all four fixed white faces were screaming horribly, silently, forever. The franchise's staff and customers, freed from their imposed fears, now had something real to be afraid of. They screamed and howled and ran for the open door. I hauled Suzie back out of the way as they stampeded past us, fighting and clawing each other in their need to get away. I felt very much like joining them. The sheer presence of the angel was viscerally disturbing, like every authority figure you ever knew was out to get you, all rolled into one.

I've never got on well with authority figures.

The angel gestured with a brightly glowing hand, and one of the salt statues toppled over and shattered. Suzie slapped me hard on the arm to get my attention.

"The Gun, Taylor. Give me the Gun, dammit. Give me the Speaking Gun!"

Her voice was back under control, but her eyes were fey and wild. "No," I said. "I get to try it first."

I yanked the case out of my inner coat pocket. It

felt unpleasantly warm to the touch. I snapped open
the lid and took out the Speaking Gun. The case fell
unnoticed to the floor as I stood paralysed, unable to
move even the smallest part of me. My skin crawled,
revulsed at contact with the Gun made of meat. It was
like holding the hand of someone long dead, but still
horribly, eagerly active. It felt hot and sweaty and
feverish. It felt sick and powerful. The Speaking Gun
had woken up. It breathed wetly in my hand, and its
slow heavy thoughts crawled sluggishly across the
front of my mind. The Gun was awake, and it wanted
to be used. On everything. It ached to say the back-
ward Words that would uncreate all the material
world. It had been made to destroy angels, but its ap-
petite had grown down the many, many years. And
yet the Gun was dependent on others to use it, to pull
its trigger formed from a tooth, and it *hated* that.
Hated me. Hated everything that lived. The Speaking
Gun forced its filthy thoughts upon me, determined to
control and compel me, to make me its weapon. Its
thoughts and feelings were in no way human. It was
as though death and decay and destruction had found
a voice, and hideous ambition. It knew my Name, and
ached to say it.

It took all my self-control, all my rigid self-discipline,
and all the outrage raised in me by the Bedlam Boys, to
force my fingers open one at a time, until the Speaking Gun fell stickily from my hand and hit the floor,
still howling defiantly in my mind. I shut it out, be-

hind my strongest shields, and leaned back against the wall behind me, shaking and shuddering.

The angel was gone. It had seen the Speaking Gun, and that was enough.

The restaurant was quiet now. The staff and customers were gone, the angel had escaped, and the Bedlam Boys were salt. There was just me and Suzie. My whole body was shaking, my hands beating a noisy tattoo against the wall. My mind felt like it had been violated. I could feel tears running down my cheeks. Walker had been right. Some cures are far worse than the diseases. I looked down at the Gun on the floor, lying beside its case, but I couldn't bring myself to reach down and touched the damned thing. So Suzie knelt and did it for me, closing the case around the Gun without actually touching it herself. She slipped the case into her jacket pocket, then stood patiently beside me while I got myself under control again. It was the closest she could come to comforting me.

Soon enough the shuddering stopped, and I was myself again. I felt tired, bone tired and soul tired, as though I hadn't slept for a week. I wiped the drying tears off my face with my hands, sniffed a few times, and gave Suzie my best reassuring smile. It felt fairly convincing. Suzie took it in the spirit with which it was intended and nodded briskly, all business again. Suzie's always been uncomfortable around naked emotions.

"I'll carry the case," she said. "I'm more used to guns than you are."

"It isn't just a gun, Suzie."

She shrugged. "That angel. Do you think it was from Above or Below?"

It was my turn to shrug. "Does it matter, Suzie? When the Bedlam Boys had us, trapped in our fears, for a moment I saw what you saw . . ."

"We won't talk about that," Suzie said flatly. "Not now. Not ever. If you are my friend."

Sometimes being a friend means knowing when to let things go and shut the hell up. So I pushed myself away from the wall and headed for the nearest of the three remaining salt statues. Suzie followed after me. The scattered remains of the shattered statue crunched loudly under our feet. I looked at the three white faces, trapped in a moment of horror, forever. Sometimes I think the whole universe runs on irony.

"Well, there goes our chances of finding the Collector's location," said Suzie, her voice and face utterly calm and easy.

"Not necessarily," I said. "Remember the first rule of the private detective, when in doubt, check their pockets for clues."

"I thought the first rule was wait until the client's cheque has cleared?"

"Picky picky."

It took a while, but eventually we turned up a single embossed business card, proclaiming a perfor-

mance by Nasty Jack Starlight at the old Styx Theatre, dated that very day. Or, more properly, night.

"So Starlight's back in town," I said. "Wouldn't
have thought he was the Boys' cup of tea."

"Has to be a connection," said Suzie. "I know for a
fact that Starlight's supposed to have supplied certain
items to the Collector in the past."

"Let's go talk to the man," I said. "See what he
knows."

"Let's," said Suzie. "I'm in the mood to talk
forcibly to someone. Possibly even violently."

"Never knew a time when you weren't," I said
generously.

We walked through the streets of the Nightside,
through a city under siege. There were angels everywhere now, soaring across the night sky, plunging
down to snatch victims right out of the street, spreading terror and destruction. There were screams and
cries, fires and explosions. Dark plumes of smoke
rose from burning buildings on all sides. People had
been driven out into the streets, as homes and businesses and hiding places collapsed into rubble behind
them. Everywhere I looked there were salt statues,
and bodies impaled on lamp-posts. Burned and blackened corpses lay piled up in the gutters, and once I
saw someone turned inside out, still horribly alive
and suffering. Suzie put him out of his misery. Judge-

ment Day had come to the Nightside, and it wasn't pretty. There was gun-fire all over the place, and fiery explosions, and now and again I felt the fabric of the world shake as some poor desperate fool levelled heavy-duty magics against the invading angels. Nothing stopped them, or even slowed them down. Grey men in grey suits stood unnaturally still in doorways, or looked out of alleyways, or walked untouched out of fire-gutted buildings. They were everywhere, and people ran howling before them, driven like cattle to the slaughter.

Suzie and I hadn't been out in the street five minutes before an angel came swooping down out of the night sky, brilliant as a falling star, fierce and irrevocable, blazing wings spread wide, heading straight for me. I gave it my best significant glare, but it kept coming. Suzie pulled the Speaking Gun's case out of her jacket, and the angel changed course immediately, sweeping over our heads and flashing down the street behind us like a snow-white comet. Suzie and I stopped and looked at each other. Suzie weighed the case in her hand.

"Guess word about the Speaking Gun has got around."

"So much for the element of surprise," I said.

She sniffed. "I'd rather have the element of naked threat any day."

We started off down the street again, walking unhurriedly while everyone else ran, and blood and chaos flowed around us. Suzie put the Gun's case away again, then unconsciously rubbed that hand against her jacket, over and over, as though trying to clean it.

The Styx was an old, abandoned theatre, set well back from the main drag, in one of the quieter back-waters of the Nightside. There are enough dramas in the Nightside's everyday life that most people don't feel any need for the theatre, but we have to have somewhere for vain and bitchy people to show off in public. Suzie and I stopped outside the large, slumping building and studied it cautiously from a safe distance. It didn't look like much. The whole of the boarded-up front was plastered with peeling, overlapping posters for local rock groups, political meetings, and religious revivals. The once proud sign above the double doors was choked with grime and dirt.

Property doesn't normally stay untenanted long in the Nightside; someone's always got a use for it. But this place was different. Some thirty years ago, some poor fool tried to open a Gate to Hell during a performance of the Caledonian Tragedy, and that kind of thing plays havoc with property values. The three witches killed and ate the guy responsible, but didn't have the skills to close what he'd partway opened. The Authorities had to bring in an outside troubleshooter, one Augusta Moon, and while she sewed the thing up tighter than a frog's arse, the incident still left a nasty taste in everyone's spiritual mouth.

Even unsuccessful Hellgates can affect the tone of a whole neighbourhood.

Unsurprisingly enough, the theatre's double doors were locked, so Suzie kicked them in, and we strolled nonchalantly into the lobby. It was dirty and dusty, with thick shrouds of cobwebs everywhere. The shadows were very dark, and the still air smelled stale and sour. Dust motes swirled slowly in the shafts of light that had followed us in through the open door, as though they were disturbed by the light's intrusion. The once plush carpet was dry and crunchy under our feet. The whole place reeked of faded nostalgia, of better times long gone. It was like walking back into the shadows of the past. Old posters advertising old productions still clung stubbornly to the walls, faded and fly-specked. The Patchwork Players Present: Marlowe's *King Lier,* Webster's *Revenger's Triumph,* Ibsen's *Salad Days.* There was no sign anyone had been here for thirty years.

"Odd name for a theatre," Suzie said finally, her voice echoing loudly in the quiet. "What's a Styx, when it's at home?"

"The Styx is a river that runs through Hell," I said. "Made up from the tears shed by suicides. Sometimes it bothers me that I know things like that. Maybe the theatre specialised in tragedies. We may be in the wrong place, Suzie. Look around you. No-one's disturbed this dust in years."

"In which case," said Suzie, "where's that music coming from?"

I listened carefully, and sure enough, faint strains of music were coming from somewhere up ahead. Suzie drew her shotgun, and we crossed the lobby and made our way up to the stage doors. The music was definitely louder. We pushed the doors open and stepped through into the theatre proper. It was very dark, and we stood there for a while till our eyes adjusted. Up on the stage, in two brilliant following spotlights was Nasty Jack Starlight with his life-sized living rag doll partner, singing and dancing.

The music was an old sixties classic, the Seekers' "The Carnival Is Over." Nasty Jack Starlight sang along cheerfully, stepping it out across the dusty stage with more style than precision. He was dressed as Pierrot, in a Harlequin suit of black and white squares, and his face was made up to resemble a grinning skull, with dark, hollowed eyes and white teeth painted on his smiling lips, all of it topped with a jaunty sailor's cap. He was tall and gangling, and he danced with more deliberation than grace as his voice soared along with the melancholy song.

He danced a fiercely merry two-step with his partner, a living rag doll costumed as Columbine. She was almost as tall as he was, her arms and legs amazingly flexible as she danced, without joints to get in the way. She had a sadly erotic look, in her patched dress of many colours, and her face of tightly stretched white satin had garishly painted-on features. Her movements were disturbingly sexual, her dance provocative in every lascivious movement.

Pierrot and Columbine capered across the whole stage, making the most of the space, dancing and leaping and pirouetting in the two spotlights that followed them faithfully wherever they went. I looked back and above me, but there was no sign anywhere of a source for the spotlights. They just were. The music also seemed to come from nowhere. It changed abruptly to "Sweet Little Jazz Baby, That's Me," a staple from the Roaring Twenties, and Pierrot and Columbine came together and Charlestoned for all they were worth. Their feet on the stage made no sound at all. The music had a distorted, eerily echoing quality, as though it had had to travel a long way to get there and lost something of itself along the way. And for all the effort Nasty Jack Starlight and his partner put into their performance, it all had a dull, flat feeling. There was no appeal to it, no charisma or emotion. But the packed audience was in ecstatics, sheer raptures of emotion.

The audience.

Nasty Jack Starlight and his living rag doll were singing and dancing for the dead. Now that my eyes had adjusted to the gloom, I could see the stalls were full of zombies, vampires, mummies, werewolves, and ghosts of varying density. Every form of undead or half-life the Nightside had to offer, all come together in one place under a strict pact of non-aggression that wouldn't have lasted five minutes anywhere else. But no-one would destroy the truce here; no-one would dare. This was the one place they could come to recapture just a little of their lost or discarded humanity. To remember what it felt like to be alive.

The vampires looked right at home in their formal tuxedos and ball gowns, daintily sipping blood from discreet thermoses, passed back and forth. In comparison, the mummies looked distinctly drab and dirty in their yellowing bandages, and dust puffed out when they clapped their hands together. The werewolves huddled together in a clump, howling along to the tune, their alpha male distinguished by an impressive leather jacket made from human hide, the tattooed words on its back proclaiming him Leader of the Pack. The ghouls mostly kept to themselves, snacking on fingers from a takeaway tub. The zombies tended to sit very still, and applauded very carefully, in case anything dropped off. They sat as far away from the ghouls as possible. The ghosts varied from full manifestations to pale misty shapes, some so thinly spread their hands passed through each other when they tried to clap along. Others had to concentrate all their sense of personality just to keep from falling through their chairs. But dead, undead, partly human, or mostly inhuman, they all seemed to be having a good time.

They laughed and cheered, sighed and wept, and applauded in unison, as though reacting to what was happening on the stage, though their responses seemed to have little to do with the performance.

Nasty Jack Starlight performed exclusively for the dead, or those feeling distanced from their original humanity. He remembered old emotions for them, evoked them through his singing and dancing, and *made* his audience feel them. He made them feel alive again, if only fleetingly. His patrons paid very well for the illusion of life he gave them, for a while . . . and while they wallowed in second-hand emotions, Starlight fed off their unnatural vitality, sucking it out of them as he danced, gorging on their inhuman energies like a happy little parasite. He had lived many lifetimes in this fashion, and intended to live many more. Long ago, he'd made a really bad deal with Something he was still afraid to name aloud, and now he couldn't afford to die. Ever.

I had to explain all this to Suzie. She'd never had any interest in the theatre. At the end, she sniffed, unimpressed.

"So what's the deal with the rag doll?" she said.

"The word is she was human once, and Jack Starlight's lover. He needed a dancing partner, but he didn't feel at all inclined to share what he'd be taking from his audience. So he had her made over into what she is now. A living rag doll, endlessly compliant, a partner who'll follow his every move and whim, and never complain. Of course, that was a long time ago . . . She's probably quite insane by now. If she's lucky. Now you know why they call him *Nasty* Jack Starlight."

"Who was she, originally?" said Suzie, glaring at the stage.

"No-one knows who she was any more. Except Jack, of course, and he'll never tell. Nasty little man that he is. Come on, let's go on up and ruin his day."

"Let's. I might even ruin his posture while I'm at it."

We strode off down the central aisle, side by side. The dead in the seats nearest us didn't even glance round as we passed, utterly transfixed by the performance onstage, and the old emotions flooding through what was left of their hearts. There was magic in the air, and it had nothing to do with sorcery. On and on they danced, Pierrot and Columbine, Harlequin and his rag doll, never stopping or resting as the music changed inexorably from one sentimental ditty to another . . . as though they had no need to pause, to refresh their strength or regain their breath. And perhaps they didn't. He was feeding, and she . . . she was just a rag doll, after all, her wide eyes and smiling lips only painted on. Neither of them suffered from human limitations any more. They mimed love and tenderness for their audience, and meant none of it.

It was all just an act.

Suzie and I vaulted up onto the stage, and everything stopped. The music cut off, and Starlight and his rag doll immediately ended their dance. They each stood very still in their separate spotlights, as Suzie and I approached them. Nasty Jack Starlight struck an elegant pose, calm and relaxed, smiling his skullface smile while his eyes gleamed brightly from darkened hollows. The rag doll had frozen in mid move, her head turned away, her arms and legs interrupted at impossible angles, inhumanly flexible. The audience was still only for a moment as the performance was interrupted, then they burst out into a roar of boos and yells and insults, quickly descending into open threats and menaces. Suzie glared out at them, to little effect. I turned and gave them my best thoughtful stare, and everyone shut up.

"I'm impressed," Suzie said quietly.

"To tell the truth, so am I," I said. "But don't tell them that. Jack Starlight! It's been a while, hasn't it, Jack? You still on your world tour of the Nightside?"

"Still playing to packed houses," Starlight said easily. "And they say the theatre's dead . . ." His voice was soft and precise, completely without accent or background. He could have been from anywhere, anywhen. His unwavering smile was very wide, and his eyes never blinked. "You know, most hecklers have the decency to do it from their seats. What do you want, Taylor? You are interrupting genius at work."

"We found your card in the possession of one of the Bedlam Boys," I said. "They worked for the Collector."

"I notice you're using the past tense. Am I to presume the little shits are all dead? My my, Taylor, you have become hard-core since your return."

"Tell me about the card, Jack," I said, deliberately not correcting his presumption. "What's your connection with the Collector?"

He shrugged easily enough. "There's not much to tell. The Collector sent the Boys round to lean on me, because he'd heard I once very nearly got my hands on the Unholy Grail, some years ago in France. I was excavating at Rennes-le-Château, in search of the Maltese Falcon . . ."

I winced. "I thought you had more sense, Jack. Never go after the Maltese Falcon. That's the first rule of private investigators."

Suzie frowned. "I thought the first rule was . . ."

"Not now, Suzie. Continue, Jack."

"Well, imagine my surprise when my companions unwrapped the contents of the hidden grave, and we found ourselves face to face with the Unholy Grail. It all got rather unpleasant after that. It's always sad when friends fall out over money. . . . Anyway, after the dust had settled and the blood had dried, I ended up having to leave the chateau empty-handed, and at speed. But I still remain one of the few men who has actually seen the Unholy Grail with his own eyes, and lived to tell of it."

"What did it look like?" said Suzie.

Nasty Jack Starlight considered for a moment. "Cold. Ugly. Seductive. I wasn't stupid enough to touch it, even then. I know evil when I see it."

"You should," I said. "You've had enough practice. So, what did you tell the Bedlam Boys, when they came calling?"

He laughed softly. It was a dark, unpleasant sound. "I didn't tell them a damned thing. I kicked their over-padded arses and sent them home crying to their master. Teach the Collector to set his dogs on me. Their fears were no match for my emotions. I am a master of my craft, and don't you forget it. And that is it. There's nothing more I can tell you about the Unholy Grail or the Collector. Just ships that passed in the Nightside, that's all. Now, do either of you happen to be in show business? Then perhaps you'll both be good enough to get the hell off my stage. I am making art here. Why is there never a guy with a long hook around when you need him?"

"There are angels all over the Nightside," I said. "They're looking for anyone with any knowledge of, or connection to, the Unholy Grail. And they're not playing nicely. They don't have to. They're angels. Now, impressive though your audience is, the whole lot of them put together wouldn't be enough to even slow down an angel. Even if they did feel disposed to try and protect you, which I personally doubt. The dead can be so fickle. On the other hand, you help us track down the Unholy Grail, and/or the Collector, and Suzie and I will protect you."

Nasty Jack Starlight shook his head slowly. "Just when you think it can't get any worse . . . Angels in the Nightside. Right! That is it. I am out of here." He turned to face the audience. "Ladies and gentlemen, tonight's show is cancelled on account of Biblical intervention. Good night, God bless, hope it was good for you too. Form an orderly queue for the exits. Sorry, no refunds."

He stalked over to his rag doll partner, snapped his fingers sharply, and she collapsed limply over his waiting shoulder, as though there was nothing inside her but straw and stuffing. And perhaps there wasn't. Certainly she seemed no weight at all to Starlight as he headed determinedly for the wings. I didn't see any point in trying to stop him. He didn't have anything I needed, and an unwilling partner would only slow us down. But then Nasty Jack Starlight stopped abruptly, turned round and looked back, moving slowly, almost reluctantly. And that was when we all realised there was someone else onstage with us. We looked slowly at the back of the stage, even the rag doll raising her satin face. There, standing behind us, still and silent like a living shadow, was a grey man in a grey suit.

He waited till we were all looking, then he blazed

like the sun, a light so bright it was painful to merely human eyes. Suzie and I stumbled back, shielding our faces with upraised arms. Starlight turned and ran for the edge of the stage. The rag doll hanging down over his shoulder was the only one to stare adoringly at the angel, with her dark-painted eyes. The audience was in a panic, shrieking and crying out in alarm, while the word *angel* moved swiftly among them like a curse. Ghosts disappeared, snapping out of existence like popping soap bubbles. Vampires became bats and flapped away. Those still burdened with material bodies fought their way out into the aisles and sprinted for the lobby doors.

The angel became a pillar of fire in human form, spreading wide his glowing wings, brilliant and terrible and incandescent with glory. There was a stench of burning flesh and melting metals. The rag doll hanging limply over Starlight's shoulder burst into flames. They leapt up impossibly fast, consuming the doll from head to toe. And still she stared adoringly through the flames at the angel. Starlight cried out in pain and rage, and threw her from him. She flopped about on the stage, burning fiercely. She tried to crawl towards Starlight, but the flames were too hot, too eager, and she was only rags and stuffing. She burned up, and she was gone, and in moments there was nothing left of her but a scorch mark on the stage, and dark smoke drifting slowly though the air. It smelled of violets.

Starlight didn't spare the burning doll a glance once he'd thrown her aside. He ran for the edge of the stage, and had almost made it when his clothes burst into flames. The sailor's cap went up first, burning fiercely with a pale blue flame, setting his hair on fire. Then the Harlequin's costume caught alight, flames leaping everywhere at once. He beat at the flames with his bare hands, but soon they were burning too. In a matter of seconds, his whole body was burning hotter than a furnace. He screamed once, and a long jet of yellow flame shot out of his mouth from his burning lungs. He fell forward onto the stage, and lay there kicking and jerking, while the flames leapt even higher. They quickly consumed Nasty Jack Starlight, until there was nothing left but a few charred and blackened bones, and sizzling melted fat dripping slowly off the edge of the stage.

By that time, Suzie Shooter had the Speaking Gun out of its case, and was holding it rock steady in her hand, aimed right at the angel. But I could see from her twisted features that she was feeling the same sick horror at the Gun's touch that I had. Her iron self-control fought off its attempt to seize control of her mind, but her whole body was shaking from the effort of the struggle, even while the hand holding the Gun remained perfectly steady. All she had to do was pull the trigger. But she couldn't spare enough willpower to do it.

The angel turned its gaze away from Starlight's re-

mains and looked at Suzie. It saw the Speaking Gun
in her hand, and in a moment it was gone, flying up-
wards on wings of dazzling brightness, crashing
through the roof of the theatre and up and out into the
safety of the night skies.

Suzie didn't move, still aiming the Speaking Gun
at where the angel had been. Her face was pale, and
slick with sweat. Her eyes were fixed and wild. Her
whole body was shaking now, as she and the Gun
fought for control of her mind, and her soul. And in
the end she won, and threw the Gun from her. Perhaps because in the end she was Shotgun Suzie, who
owned guns, and not the other way round. She won,
and I never knew how much it cost her. I never
asked. Because what she did tell me was so much
worse.

She sat down suddenly on the stage, as though her
legs had just given out. Her hands twitched meaning-
lessly in her lap, and she rocked back and forth like a
troubled child. She wasn't crying; she was beyond
that. Her eyes were wild, desperate, feral. She was
making a low, moaning sound, like an animal in pain.
I sat down beside her, and put an arm round her
shoulders to comfort her. She shrieked dismally, and
scuttled away from me like a child afraid of a beating.
I moved cautiously after her, careful not to get too
close.

"It's all right, Suzie," I said. "I'm here. It's over.
Let me help you."

"You can't," she said, not looking at me.

"I'm here . . . it's me, John."

"But you can't touch me," she said, her voice so harsh now it was almost inhuman. "No-one can. I can't bear to be touched, by anyone. Not ever again. Can't be vulnerable, to anyone."

I knelt before her, trying to hold her darting gaze with mine. I was desperate to help her, to haul her back from the edge, but it felt like the wrong choice of words might shatter her into so many pieces, she'd never recover. I'd never seen her like this before. So . . . defenceless.

"When the Bedlam Boys brought out our fears," I said slowly, "I saw what you saw. I was there with you, in the hospital. I saw . . . the baby."

"There was no baby," she said tiredly. "It has to be born to be a baby. What you saw was how the foetus looked, after I had it aborted. I left it so late because I was ashamed. Too ashamed to tell my parents that my brother had been abusing me since I was thirteen, and the baby would be his. It wasn't rape, not really. Sometimes he'd buy me things, little presents. And sometimes he'd say he'd kill me if I ever told anyone. He used me. And when the truth came out, my parents blamed me. Said I must have led him on.

"I had an abortion, just after my fifteenth birthday. No cake and candles for me that year. They made me look at the foetus, afterwards. So I wouldn't forget the lesson. Like I could ever forget. I killed my brother. Shot him dead with a gun I stole. My first gun. Pissed on his body, and then ran away to the Nightside. Been here ever since. Swore I'd never be weak and vulnerable, not ever again. I'm Shotgun Suzie now, death on two legs. But I can't be touched. Not by anyone. Not even by a friend, or a lover. I'm safe now. Safe from everyone. Even myself."

"You mean . . . there's never been anyone in your life?" I said. "No-one you could ever trust enough to . . ."

"No. Never."

"I had no idea how alone you really were, Suze."

"Don't call me that," she said in a dead voice. "That's what he used to call me."

"Oh Jesus, I'm so sorry, Suzie. I am so sorry."

Some life came back into her eyes as she looked at me, and her mouth turned down in a bitter smile. "I would trust you with my life, John. But I can't bear to have you touch me. My brother won after all. Because even though I killed him, he's always with me."

I didn't know what to say, so I just said "I'm here, Suzie."

"I know," she said. "And sometimes, that's enough."

She got up, retrieved the Speaking Gun by wrapping the case around it, and put the case back in her jacket. She stood on the edge of the stage, looking out into the darkness. She seemed entirely composed again. I came and stood beside her.

"It's just a gun," she said, not looking at me. "I know how to handle guns. Next time, I'll use it."

I nodded. And after a while we walked out of the Styx Theatre together, side by side and miles and miles between us.

We'd only just got out into the street when my mobile rang again. This time it was Razor Eddie, Punk God of the Straight Razor. Or so he claims, and since he tends to kill people who disagree, not many people contest the point any more. Certainly he's one of the strangest and most dangerous people in the Nightside, and that takes some doing. I suppose we're friends. It's hard to tell sometimes, in the Nightside. This time he had information for me.

"I hear you're looking for the Unholy Grail," he said, without preamble. "I know where it is. The Collector's got it."

"I'd pretty much worked that out for myself," I said. "What makes you think the Collector's got it?"

"Because I got it for him," said Eddie. His voice was a ghostly whisper, as always. "To be exact, he hired me to take it away from the bastards who had it. The Collector got a bit jumpy after his people lost the Speaking Gun, so he came to me. Normally he'd know better, but this time he had something I wanted, so we struck a deal. The Unholy Grail was in the hands of the Warriors of the Cross, a bunch of hard-core Christian evangelists who planned to use the Unholy Grail's power to launch a Crusade against the Nightside and slaughter everyone and everything that even smacked of magic. Anything that wasn't pure, untainted human was to be exterminated as ungodly and unchristian. Since that definitely included me, I was only too happy to get my own pre-emptive strike in first."

"The Collector hired you?" I said. "I didn't think you had any use for money any more?"

"I don't," said Razor Eddie. "His payment was the current location of the Warriors of the Cross. I'd been looking for those bastards for some time. They'd been hauling teenage runaways off to their hidden base and brainwashing them, then sending them out to act as spies, and honey to trap more kids. They were going to be the cannon fodder of the Crusade."

"So the Collector definitely has the Unholy Grail now?" I said.

"Put it into his hands myself. Ugly thing. But more and more it seemed to me that he is not a fit person to have such a thing. I can't touch him. I gave my word. But I never said anything about you. So you come to me, and I'll tell you where the Collector is hiding out these days. Then you can take the damned thing away from him and put it somewhere safe. Sound good to you?"

"Best thing I've heard all day. Where are you, Eddie?"

"Back at the Warriors of the Cross's hideout, having a bit of a look round for anything else of interest."

"You mean looting," I said.

He chuckled dryly. "Old habits die hard. You know Big Sergei's Warehouse, on Kaynek Avenue?"

"I know it. Be with you in twenty minutes. You do know that there are angels in the Nightside, from Above and Below, kicking the crap out of anyone they even suspect has any connection with the Unholy Grail?"

"I don't bother them, they don't bother me," said Razor Eddie. He hung up.

I put my mobile away, and turned to Suzie. She looked as calm and composed as usual, ice-cold and perfectly poised. I filled her in on the parts of the conversation she'd missed, and she frowned.

"Why couldn't he just tell you where the Collector is over the phone?"

"Because you never know who might be listening," I said. "There's no such thing as a secure line in the Nightside. You know Big Sergei's place?"

"Can't say I do."

"He's Russian mafiosi. You want it, he can get it for you. Guns and armour a speciality, which is presumably why the Warriors of the Cross went to him. You'll like him, Suzie, if Razor Eddie's left anything of him."

"You know all the best people, Taylor. Let's go. I want to get this case over with."

"Suzie . . ."

"Let's go."

So we went, together, once more side by side.

#

Death Comes Suddenly

Suzie and I hurried through largely deserted streets, while fires burned all across the Nightside, like warning balefires set against the dark. The air was thick with smoke and drifting ashes, and the smell of bodies burning. Buildings exploded, blown apart by angelic light, like party favours in Hell. There were so many angels flying overhead now that they blocked out most of the light from the moon and the stars. Most of the street-lights were smashed. The Nightside was at its lowest ebb, illuminated mostly by the leaping flames of its own destruction. Suzie and I stuck to the shadows and sprinted through the shifting pools of light. The streets seemed eerily still and quiet without the usual massed traffic rushing endlessly past, but everyone who could leave the Nightside was long gone by now, and no-one outside was stupid enough to come in.

Angels had come to the Nightside, from Above and Below, and the night had never seemed so dark.

Down in Time Tower Square, some of the area's major players had come out into the streets, out into the open, to make a last stand against the invading forces. Suzie and I watched from the shadows of a recessed doorway and hoped not to be noticed. The Lord of Thorns stood proudly with his staff of power, cut from the Tree of Life itself. Lightning crackled around him, and he laughed like a crow on a battlefield as angels wheeled away rather than meet his baleful gaze. Count Video leaned casually against a lamp-post, wrapped in static and shifting plasma lights, his pale skin studded with silicon nodes and sorcerous circuitry. He sniggered nastily as his long-fingered hands weaved binary magic, rewriting reality with applied description theory and insane mathematics, and the angels couldn't get anywhere near him. King of Skin slouched into the Square, his eyes bright with glory, undoing probabilities with his terrible glamour. And Bloody Blades, reeking of sweat and musk and awful appetites, snorted and stamped his great hooves impatiently as he waited for one of the others to bring something down in reach of his great spurred hands.

And all through Time Tower Square there was a terrible sound of angels crying out in pain and rage, as magic moved in the night, denying them their rightful prey.

The angels flew in great spirals overhead, moving faster and faster, spreading wider and wider as they gathered in ever greater numbers. Soon there would be so many of them that no amount of magics would be enough to hold them back, then they would descend. One had clearly been impatient, and had paid the price. It had ventured too low, too soon, and one of the major players had snatched it out of the air and crucified it against the side of the Time Tower. Dozens of cold iron nails pierced its outstretched arms and legs, pinning it to the wall like a frog in a science lab, ready for dissection. But the angel was still alive, its light flickering feebly like a fallen star. Its golden eyes wept slow, mystified tears, unable to understand what had brought it so low. It was finding out the limitations of the material world the hard way. Its severed wings lay on the ground beneath its broken feet.

Further off in the night, in a direction that could not be named or pointed to, there was a sound like a great engine slowly turning, as older, darker, more powerful presences began to wake, to defend the Nightside. They stirred in ancient vaults, or long-forgotten graves, creatures and beings of power and legend, some of them almost as old as angels, and as dreadful.

The Nightside is an old, old place.

Suzie and I eased around the edges of the Square, scurrying from one place of relative safety to the next. The air was full of the stresses of great forces clashing, like icebergs grinding together in the night sea. I had no intention of getting involved. I knew when I was out of my depth, and for once Suzie had enough sense to follow my lead. There were powers abroad in the night now that could crush both of us like bugs and never even notice. It seemed to take forever to creep around two sides of the Square, my heart hammering painfully fast in my chest all the way, but finally we were able to slip away into a blessedly anonymous side street and run for our lives. Behind us someone was screaming, but we didn't pause to look back. We weren't far from Big Sergei's Warehouse now.

And, of course, Razor Eddie. Punk God of the Straight Razor. Possibly. Sometimes a friend, sometimes not. Saint *and* sinner, all wrapped up in one enigmatic and distinctly unhygienic bundle. Your connection to minor deities and divinity wannabes, and as much trouble as you can handle. An extremely disturbing agent for the good, and no, the good didn't get any say in the matter. He lived a life of violent penance for earlier misdeeds. Lots of them. The last

time I'd seen Eddie was in a possible future I'd ac-
cessed through a Timeslip, and I'd ended up having to
kill him. It had been a mercy killing, made necessary
at least partly because of the time-travelling Collector, but even so it wasn't the kind of thing that came
up easily in the conversation. I was still trying to decide just how much, if any, of this I should tell Eddie.
The situation was complicated by Eddie's future self
blaming me for the eventual destruction of the world.
If I told Eddie that, I could quite easily see him
killing me on the spot, on general principle. Of
course, the future I'd visited wasn't inevitable. Nothing is set in stone where Time is concerned.

As in so many things, I decided the best thing to do
was wait and see what happened, and decide then, if
at all. I'd always had a real talent for putting things
off till later. Hell, I could dither for the Olympics.

Suzie and I stopped at the edge of the warehouse
district and looked cautiously about us. Fires were
burning all around, some of them seriously out of
control. The shadows danced and leapt, but the area
seemed abandoned by mortals and angels. The fighting was over, and the struggle had moved on, leaving
only flames and devastation behind. The air was tight
and hot as a summer's day, and twice as sweaty. I
could see Big Sergei's Warehouse at the end of the
street, just another anonymous building among many.
It seemed to have survived pretty much intact. The
way to it seemed clear enough, but still I hung back,

taking my time. Razor Eddie wasn't above luring me into a trap if he felt it served a higher purpose. Suzie growled restlessly at my side, hefting her pump-action shotgun and looking frustrated because she didn't have anyone to use it on.

"This whole situation stinks, Taylor." Her voice was as cold and calm as ever, but her knuckles were white from holding the shotgun too tightly. I should really have insisted she go home, and rest and recover, but I didn't because I needed her. She sniffed at the smoky air as though she could smell trouble, and perhaps she could, at that. "Think about it. Why would the Collector tell Eddie his most preciously guarded secret, the location of his collection? Eddie's spooky, but the Collector would slit his own granny's throat for a bargain. I can't see him putting his hoard at risk without a hell of a good reason. And everyone knows the Collector never gives away anything he can sell."

"True," I said. "But on the other hand, Razor Eddie isn't an easy person to say no to. More to the point, if the Collector really has been forced to reveal the location of his warehouse, you can bet he's already making plans to move his hoard to a new location. If we take too long getting the information from Eddie, it might well turn out to be worthless."

"It'll take the Collector time to move," said Suzie. "If he really does have everything he's supposed to have, it'll take him ages to shift it all. Particularly if he doesn't want to draw attention. And that's assuming he has an alternative safe site ready to move his collection to. No, we've got time. I'm more concerned with how much longer we can afford to spend standing around here. I'm beginning to feel like I've got a target painted on me. Find me something I can shoot."

She was right, of course. In times like these, doing nothing can be just as dangerous as doing the wrong thing. So I started off down the street, heading straight for Big Sergei's Warehouse, as though I didn't have a care in the world. Suzie rather spoiled the effect by slinking along beside me, gun at the ready, glaring about her like a junkyard dog. No-one shot at us, or swooped down out of the sky on glowing wings.

The front of Big Sergei's Warehouse was a long blank wall, with no name or sign anywhere. Big Sergei didn't believe in advertising. Either you knew his reputation, or you weren't big-league enough to do business with him. I kept my eyes open as we headed for the front door, ready to duck and weave and run as necessary. The warehouse was supposed to be protected by all kinds of state-of-the-art defences, everything from tailored curses to anti-aircraft guns. No-one stole from Big Sergei and lived to boast of it. Didn't stop people trying, though. This was the Nightside, after all. The front door was said to be six inches of solid steel, protected by the very finest electronic locks, and all the windows had bulletproof glass and steel shutters. Big Sergei believed in feeling secure.

Not that any of that would stop Razor Eddie, of course.

"If Big Sergei's got any sense, he'll have sealed this place up tighter than a duck's arse and gone into hiding," said Suzie. "In which case, how are we going to get in?"

"We'll just have to improvise," I said, trying hard to sound confident.

"Ah yes," said Suzie. "Improvise. Suddenly and violently and without remorse. I feel better already."

"Unfortunately," I said, slowing thoughtfully as we approached the front door, "it would appear someone else has beaten us to that."

Up close, it was clear the warehouse had taken a battering. Several of the windows had been smashed, which couldn't have been easy with bulletproof glass, and their steel shutters were buckled, hanging crookedly, or completely missing. There was a hole in the wall up by the first floor, as though it had been hit by a cannon-ball. Or a very angry fist. And the celebrated front door, six inches of solid steel protected by all kinds of heavy-duty defences, had been ripped right out of its frame and was currently lying in the street some distance away, in a severely crumpled condition. I gave it plenty of room as I cautiously approached the opening where the door had been. Suzie stuck close to me, shotgun at the ready. I peered in, satisfied myself that there was no movement or sounds of life, then stepped warily forward into the reception lobby. Suzie crowded past me, sweeping her gun back and forth, eager for a target. The possibility of imminent violence had cheered her up considerably.

The lobby was a mess. Every stick of furniture had been wrecked or overturned, and in some cases reduced to little more than kindling. The expensive carpeting had been torn and rucked up, as though whole armies had trampled across it. There were signs of bullet and bomb damage on some of the walls, and a tall potted plant in the corner had been pretty much shredded. The sheer extent of the destruction might almost have been funny, if it hadn't been for the blood. There was spilled blood everywhere, gallons of it. The torn carpeting was soaked from wall to wall, most of still so wet it squelched under our feet. There was more blood splashed across the walls, in thick red swatches and spatters, and the occasional handprint. It dripped from the shattered furniture, and from a wide wet stain on the ceiling. I didn't even want to think about what could have caused blood to jet almost a dozen feet into the air. I stepped around the dripping ceiling and advanced slowly across the lobby. I glanced at Suzie.

"If I didn't know better, I'd swear you'd been here."

She sniffed unhappily. "No, this is Razor Eddie's work. I'm a professional, he's . . . enthusiastic. You know what worries me the most about this? Lots of blood . . . but no bodies. What the hell has he done with the bodies? And what's with all this religious stuff on the walls?"

She gestured at the paintings hanging crookedly on the walls. They all depicted extremely detailed scenes from the deaths of Christian martyrs, with the emphasis very much on blood and gore and suffering. There were large crucifixes too. Extremely graphic crucifixes. And there were signs in ugly block lettering; *Pray for mercy while you still can. Every day, God is judging you. No mercy for the ungodly. The Church's way is the only way. Have you killed an unbeliever today?*

"Hard-core," said Suzie.

"None of that was here the last time I had occasion to have words with Big Sergei," I said. "He believed in profits, not prophets. I can only assume that the Warriors of the Cross wanted to buy so much from him that it was easier for him to rent them the whole warehouse, for as long as they were here. And they . . . made themselves at home. Just how many guns were the Warriors buying, I wonder?"

Suzie scowled. "Didn't he realise they were planning an invasion of the Nightside?"

I shrugged. "If he had, he wouldn't have cared. As long as they paid in advance. Someone was going to make a profit anyway, so why not him?" I looked around at all the blood and destruction. "The Unholy Grail has a lot to answer for. Jude said it attracted evil."

Suzie looked at me. "Jude?"

"Our client."

"Oh yeah. So much has happened, I'd almost forgotten about him. So, where do we go now, Taylor?"

"I think I may have spotted a clue," I said. She looked where I pointed. By a door marked STAIRS, someone had drawn a large arrow, painted in blood. "The stairs lead up to the offices on the third floor. We'd better get a move on. Razor Eddie's waiting for us."

"Wonderful," said Suzie.

We made our way up the stairs, following bloody arrows on the walls. Suzie took the lead with gun at the ready, checking every shadowed corner before she committed herself. There were no nasty surprises, only more damage and even more blood. A hell of a lot of people had to have died here, and recently, given how wet the blood still was. But there was never any sign of a body. The smeared scarlet arrows eventually led us to a small office at the back of the third floor. The door had been kicked in and was hanging drunkenly from one hinge. Suzie and I ducked past it, into the office. The cheap but practical furniture was still intact, but there was a long splash of blood across one wall. Not far away, there was a wall safe, with its heavy steel door torn away and left discarded on the floor. And sitting behind the office desk, slowly working his way through a pile of papers he'd taken from the safe, was Razor Eddie. He didn't look up as we came in.

"Hello, John. Suzie. Come on in. Make yourselves at home. Be with you in a minute."

Suzie headed straight for the open safe, grinned widely on finding it still packed with bundles of cash, and immediately set about transferring as many of them as she could into the many pockets of her leather jacket. Suzie had always been a deeply practical person.

The Punk God of the Straight Razor looked much the same as always, a painfully thin presence in an oversized grey coat that had seen better days, a really long time ago. It was torn and ragged, and apparently only held together by accumulated filth and grease. His long gaunt face was unhealthily pale, all dark hollows and fever-bright eyes. His voice was low, controlled, almost ghostly. And he smelled really bad, all the time. There are sewer rats dying of the Black Death that smell better than Razor Eddie. The only reason he didn't attract flies was because they tended to drop dead if they got too close to him. His slender pale hands moved slowly and methodically through the papers before him, now and again setting one aside in a separate pile.

"The Warriors of the Cross are an extreme, far-right Christian sect," Eddie said finally, still not looking up from what he was doing. "Widespread, very well funded, and very much into fire and brimstone and Crusades against . . . well, anything with even the faintest hint of fun about it. This particular branch of the Warriors was planning a full-scale invasion of the Nightside, in search of the Unholy Grail. Big Sergei apparently sold them everything from left-over Tiger Tanks to shoulder-mounted rocket launchers, and more guns and ammunition than the mind can comfortably comprehend, then disappeared sharpish before the shit could hit the fan. Nasty bastards, the Warriors. According to what I've found here, they were planning to set the Nightside on fire, then shoot everything that moved until someone handed over the Unholy Grail. But they got lucky. Someone just walked in here and offered to sell them the bloody thing. They, of course, tortured its location out of the poor bastard, then went and got it.

"And then I came here and took it from them. After a certain amount of unpleasantness.

"The Warriors of the Cross have done a lot of really nasty things in the past, and I had been looking for an excuse to make clear how displeased I was with them. It's extremists like this who give religion a bad name. They were only a small branch, of course, but I like to think I've sent a message."

"A message?" I said.

"Stay out of the Nightside, for starters." He looked up for the first time, and a smile moved briefly over his pale lips. "Wish I'd known the angels were coming. They'd probably have been even more unpleasant to the Warriors than I was. Not that I like the angels much better."

Suzie came back to join me, her jacket bulging with accumulated cash. She gave Eddie a hard look. "What did you do with the bodies, Eddie?"

He smiled again, just as briefly. "I sold them. Got a good price, too."

There are some conversations you know you don't want to pursue any further. I coughed politely, to draw Eddie's attention back to me. "You said you knew where we could find the Collector, Eddie. I really do need to see him rather urgently."

"Ah yes. The great mystery of the Nightside; the location of the Collector's secret lair. I've been there. No doubt you've been wondering why he should chose to reveal his greatest secret to the likes of me. Simple really. I didn't give him any choice. A quick tour of his collection was part of the price I demanded for retrieving the Unholy Grail from the Warriors and handing it over to him." Eddie laughed softly, a thin ghostly sound, like the wind gusting through dead branches. "I had him over a barrel, and he knew it. He was desperate at the thought of losing out on such a unique item, and I wanted to see his collection. I hadn't known he possessed the Speaking Gun, until he told me he'd lost it. Nasty weapon. I understand you have it now. If you're sensible, you'll get rid of it. The Speaking Gun has never made anyone happy or wealthy or wise. It was made to destroy, and that's all it does. Anyway, it occurred to me that if the Collector had one such weapon, he might well have others, and I wanted to know what. After all someday he might try to use them against me."

There were many things I might have said, but I chose not to. "We did try to use the Speaking Gun," I said. "It wasn't a success."

"Bloody thing's alive," said Suzie. "And vicious."

"In which case, I'm amazed you're still alive," said Eddie. "Hell, I'm impressed you're still sane."

"What was the Collector's place like?" said Suzie, sticking to the point as always.

"Big," said Eddie. "Bigger than the human mind can comfortably conceive. Floors and floors of it, packed to saturation point, including a whole load of crates he hasn't even got around to unpacking yet. He has so much stuff now, even he can't be sure of everything he's got. And, of course, he'd die before he brought in any assistance." Eddie considered for a moment. "I'll tell you this; he must have been collecting for a lot longer than any of us thought. He has some items you wouldn't believe . . ."

"Where is his lair, Eddie?" I said patiently. "And how do we get in?"

Eddie produced a computer card out of nowhere and laid it carefully on the desk before me. It was made of brass and studded with precious gems. "This card is programmed to open all his locks. The Collector shouldn't know it's missing yet, but I wouldn't wait too long before using it."

"Eddie," I said, "Where . . ."

"On the Moon," said Razor Eddie. "In a series of caverns and tunnels, dug out deep under the Sea of Tranquility. Complete with power, atmosphere, and artificial gravity. I don't know whether he had it made for him, or simply inherited it . . . Either way, he's filled it with all the comforts of home, and all kinds of defence systems, including some he apparently looted from the future. You have to admire the man's nerve . . . How you two get to the Moon, and into his lair, is unfortunately your problem. I can't help. The Collector teleported me there and back. Any questions?"

"Yes," I said. "Know any good travel agents?"

"Ah, Taylor," said a calm, familiar voice behind me. "Always ready with an inappropriate quip."

I took my time turning around. I knew that voice. It was Walker, standing magnificently at ease in the open doorway, as always every inch the cultivated city gent. Suzie had already spun round and was covering him with her shotgun. Walker tipped his bowler hat to her, then to me. He glanced at Razor Eddie, and his mouth made a brief moue of distaste before he looked back at me.

"Well, Taylor, still keeping bad company, I see. You could do so much better for yourself."

"By working for you, and the Authorities?" I gave him my best cold, menacing smile. "Walker, I wouldn't piss on the Authorities if they were on fire. They, and you, stand for everything I despise. I have my pride. Not to mention scruples."

"Yes," said Walker. "Best not to. I'm afraid I have some bad news for you, Taylor. It seems that the angels have made direct contact with my superiors in the Authorities. Which came as something of a shock, I understand. My superiors were apparently under the impression that they had made themselves unreachable . . . In any case, the angels have made it very clear that either the Authorities cooperate fully in locating and handing over the Unholy Grail, or the angels will raze the Nightside to the ground. Slaughter every living being, and leave not one stone left standing upon another. Angels aren't the most subtle of creatures, but then, I suppose they don't have to be."

"Which angels are we talking about here?" said Suzie. "The ones from Above, or Below?"

"I don't know," said Walker. "Either. Both. Does it really matter? The point is that the Authorities have far too much invested in the Nightside to allow such a threat to their interests, so they have agreed to assist the angels. To be exact, they ordered me to come and get you, Taylor. I will take you in, we'll all have a nice chat and a cup of tea, and perhaps the good biscuits, and then you will use your special gift to track down and locate the Unholy Grail. And no, you don't get a choice in the matter. Your presence is required. Don't scowl, Taylor. You get to save the Nightside from utter annihilation, and put yourself in the Authorities' good books, for once. Some people would be flattered and grateful. Now come along, dear boy. Time is of the essence."

"You think we're going to just let you walk in here and take him?" Suzie's voice was very flat and very dangerous, and her shotgun didn't waver an inch, trained on the second button of Walker's waistcoat. "I've never trusted the Authorities before, and I'm not about to start now. The angels already tried to screw with Taylor's head once, so they could get their hands on the Unholy Grail. This is the Nightside, Walker. We don't bow down to Heaven or Hell."

Walker looked at her dispassionately. "I don't have any orders about you, or Eddie. You're both free to leave and go your own ways. Unless you choose to interfere with this, in which case I really can't speak for your safety."

The tension in the room cranked up a whole other notch. Suzie was grinning unpleasantly, and Eddie was looking at Walker in a disturbingly thoughtful manner. Anyone else would have turned and run, but not Walker. He was the Authorities' voice, with the power to back it up. There were a lot of stories about Walker, and the things that he'd done, and none of them had a happy ending. I took a step forward, to bring his attention back to me. He smiled charmingly, but it didn't reach his eyes.

"Well done, Taylor. I knew I could rely on you to do the right thing, eventually."

"You assured me earlier that you trusted me to sort this one out," I said. "You said it would be best for everyone if I got to the Unholy Grail first and put it out of everyone's reach."

"Times change," Walker said calmly. "The wise man bows to the inevitable. I have my orders, and now so do you. Come along, Taylor. I don't want to have to get testy with you."

"Do you really want to go one-on-one with me, Walker?" I said, and something in my voice made his eyes narrow. "Maybe we should, just for the hell of it. Haven't you ever wondered . . . haven't you ever wanted to know if either of us is really everything our reputations make us out to be?"

Walker looked at me thoughtfully for a long moment, and I met his gaze unflinchingly. I could feel Suzie poising for action, tense as a coiled spring. And then Walker smiled his charming smile again, and shrugged. "Perhaps another time, Taylor. Are you sure I can't persuade you to come with me? There are forces at my beck and call that you really don't want to meet. And surely you wouldn't want to risk your friends being hurt?"

Suzie sniggered offensively. "Yeah, right. That'll be the day."

"Good-bye, Walker," I said. "I'm sure you can find your own way out."

Walker shook his head. "You know your father wouldn't approve of behaviour like this, John. He understood about duty and responsibility."

"You leave my father out of this! What did working for the Authorities ever do for him? And where were you when he needed you? You were supposed to be his friend! Where were you when he married my mother? Perhaps we should talk about my mother. Would you like that?"

"No," said Walker. "I wouldn't."

"No . . . no-one ever does," I said, cold and flat and bitter. "Funny, that."

Razor Eddie stood up behind his desk, and all eyes immediately went to him. He never looked like much, but just then his presence seemed to fill the room. He looked at Walker, and Walker inclined his head slightly, respectfully.

"John doesn't have to go anywhere he doesn't want to," said Razor Eddie, in a voice like a death sentence. "And don't think you can threaten me, Walker. I have known worse things than Authorities or angels."

"And I'm just plain mean," said Shotgun Suzie.

"I have seen the Unholy Grail," said Razor Eddie. "The Collector wasn't fit to have it, and neither are you, or the angels. It is a thing that doesn't belong here, and the only person I trust to get rid of it is Taylor. Go now, John, Suzie. I'll keep Walker occupied."

Walker looked at me almost sadly. "You didn't really think I'd come here alone, did you?"

A gaudily coloured blur swept past him and into the office, blasting through the open doorway almost too fast to be seen. Something buffeted me in passing, almost knocking me off my feet, and rushed on to slam into Razor Eddie. The sheer force of the impact lifted him off his feet, smashed him clean through the closed window behind him, and sent him tumbling helplessly through the smoky air to the ground three stories below. Suzie was only just turning round, and trying to bring her gun to bear, when the blur turned and swept back, and a single horribly clawed hand slapped the shotgun out of Suzie's hand, then whipped back to tear out her guts. The black leather jacket blew apart in an explosion of tatters, and Suzie cried out once, in shock and pain, as her stomach opened up like a great mouth, and her intestines fell out in a rush of blood. She collapsed to her knees, grabbing with shaky hands at the thick purple ropes spilling out of her. More blood gushed out, soaking her lap and legs, and pooling on the floor around her.

It only took a few steps before I was kneeling beside her and holding her in my arms, but it seemed to

take forever. I held her shoulders tightly, trying to
stop her shaking. Her face was bone white, and already wet with sweat. She rolled her eyes at me and
tried to say something, but her mouth was loose and
ugly and wouldn't work properly. There was no fear
in her eyes, only something that might have been a
terrible resignation. One bloody hand groped around
for her shotgun, but it was on the other side of the
room. Her other hand was still trying to stuff severed
bits of intestines back into her stomach. The stench of
blood and guts was almost overwhelming. Suzie was
breathing clumsily now, great heaving gasps, as
though every breath was an effort.

She was dying, and both of us knew it.

And then the blur came to a sudden halt before me,
solidifying into a familiar shape, one I hadn't seen in
years. I should have known; it had to be her. She
struck an elegant pose before me and smiled a happy
contented smile. She always did like to show off. In
one white-gloved hand she held the Speaking Gun's
case, taken from Suzie even as she ripped out her
guts. She waggled the case a few times before me, as
a trophy, then slipped it casually under one arm.

"A little extra, I think, on top of my exorbitant fee.
You don't object, do you, Walker darling?"

Walker started to say something, then stopped himself.

"Hello, Belle," I said, in a voice I didn't recognise.
"It's been a while, hasn't it?"

"Oh, years and years, darling. But you know me. Always happy to bump into old friends."

Belle. Short for *La Belle Dame Sans Merci*. Tall and elegant, beautiful and sophisticated, supernaturally slender. She had poise and style and vicious charm, and an aristocratic disdain for small-minded things like ethics or morality, good or evil. She was what she was, and delighted in it. Her face had a marvelous bone structure, a broad forehead, purple eyes and a heavy, sulky mouth. Belle was a freelancer—intrigue, murder, theft, and conspiracy, or anything else you might desire, as long as you could pay for it. She'd done it all in her time, and always on her own terms. She drifted from one European capital to another, leaving a trail of broken hearts and broken bodies behind her, and never once looked back. Mostly she stayed out of the Nightside. Said the place was beneath her. I think she just felt happier away from any real competition.

To give her her due, she'd always been ready to take on anyone, anywhere, and she'd never been known to lose. Mainly because Belle had armoured herself in trophies taken from her many victims. On her back she wore a werewolf's pelt, thick and grey and shaggy. She skinned the hide off him herself, and now she wore the pale grey fur all the way down her back, with the emptied head pulled forward over her head like a hood. The skull's long canines dented her forehead, above her purple eyes. It wasn't just a garment; her magics kept the pelt alive and plugged into her own system. It was her skin now, her fur, and as a result she had a werewolf's ability to regenerate. Her burnished golden breastplate was made from a dragon's hide, and it formed utterly impenetrable armour. Her shimmering white elbow-length gloves were in fact a vampire's lily white skin, flayed from the undead victim by Belle's own fair hand. On one of her hands, heavy claws pushed through the white glove; claws taken from a ghoul and fused onto her own fingers. The thigh-high leather boots were new. I didn't know who she'd got them from. Belle's magics made her various armours a part of her, made her, for all practical purposes, unkillable.

Belle was very much a self-made woman.

Most strikingly, the two halves of her face didn't match. The left half was a distinctly darker shade than the rest of her body. One victim had got close enough to rip half of Belle's face away. So after she was dead, Belle took half the victim's face as a replacement. The new skin was younger, tighter, and a perfect fit.

Belle would go anywhere, and do anyone, as long as the cheque cleared. Or as long as the enemy was a challenge, or had something Belle wanted.

I clutched Suzie to me, cradling her shaking body in my arms. She was trembling violently now, as shock took hold. Blood ran in sudden spurts from her slack mouth, and dripped off her chin. I could almost feel the life going out of her. Part of me wanted to throw myself at Belle and tear her throat out, make her pay for what she'd done. But I couldn't do that. I had to be smarter, sharper, than that. Belle was armoured against all attacks, physical or magical. Or so she thought. My only hope was to keep cool and talk calmly with Belle. Keep her mind occupied, distracted, while I slowly and very surreptitiously focussed my gift on her. Do it right, and she'd never even notice. As long as I narrowed my concentration right down, into a single cold needle, I should be able to slip my gift past her mental and magical defences just long enough to do what I had to do. It was dangerous. If Belle even suspected what I was planning, she'd have my throat out in a second, and to hell with her mission. And even so small a use of my gift would still blaze like a beacon in the night, revealing my presence to those who were always hunting me. So I had to be careful, and focussed, and utterly underhanded.

Luckily, I was good at that.

"Been a long time, Belle," I said, in something very like a normal voice. "What is it, six, seven years since we worked together on that Hellstorm business? I thought we made a good team."

"Don't try to appeal to my better nature, darling," Belle said in her marvelously cool and smoky voice. "You know very well I don't have one. We made good partners, John, but we were never more than that."

"I heard the Walking Man got you, stalking you through the catacombs under Paris."

"Oh he very nearly did, darling, but I'm so very hard to kill. Unlike your little sweetie there. Poor Suzie. Never did know what you saw in her."

"You're a lot faster than you used to be, Belle. Been taking vitamins?"

"See these new boots, darling? Aren't they simply super? I skinned a minor Greek deity to get them, so I could have his speed."

"Give it up, John," said Walker. "Come with me now, and I promise you I'll see Suzie gets help. No-one has to die here. Don't let your pride get in the way. I'm the good guy, this time. I'm saving the Nightside from destruction."

"I've been told," I said, still looking at Belle, "that if either set of angels gets their hands on the Unholy Grail, Armageddon could come early."

"You say that like it's a bad thing," said Walker. "The dark chalice doesn't belong among people, John. It's always been trouble. Let it pass to others more suited to control it."

"Ah, Walker," I said. "Always ready with an inappropriate homily." I smiled sadly at Belle. "You must know you can't trust him, or the Authorities."

"I don't trust anyone, darling. But Walker paid in advance, so I'm all his, for as long as the money lasts. And after this unfortunate business is over, and they're finished with you, I've been promised that I can root through your living brains until I find the source of your special gift. Then I'll rip it out and stick it in my own head. And your gift will become mine. Isn't that sweet? It means you'll always be with me. Now put Suzie down, dear, and come with me. Or do you want to dance a little first?"

I put Suzie carefully to one side, laying her tenderly on the bloody floor. Her eyes stayed locked on mine. I stood up and faced Belle. The whole front of my coat was soaked in Suzie's blood. More of it dripped from my clenched hands. I grinned at Belle, cold as ice. "Let's dance, darling."

She laughed in my face. "You wouldn't hit a lady, would you?"

"Sure," I said. "Know any?"

And while she was still laughing, I hit her with my sharply focussed gift, driving it right past all her defences. I can find anything, with my gift. This time, I found the single small magic that Belle used to hold all her acquisitions together, that made it possible for her to access all their various attributes. And it was the easiest thing in the world for me to tear that magic away from her and crush it with my mind. Belle screamed once as the magic vanished, and her control over her various armours disappeared with it. The werewolf pelt fell away from her back and head, revealing only bare meat showing, red and glistening, with no skin left to cover it any more. The long gloves and boots cracked and rotted and fell apart, leaving bare muscles and tendons showing on her arms and legs. And half her face, the younger half, slipped away from her head, disintegrating into dust. Belle shrieked horribly, half her face a horror show.

I stepped forward and hit her once, breaking her neck. She was dead before she hit the floor.

I leaned over her and grabbed the werewolf pelt. It started to come apart in my hands, but I thought it would hold together long enough for what I had in mind. I looked around for Walker, but he was gone. Presumably in search of reinforcements. I knelt down beside Suzie. She was lying ominously still, scarcely even breathing. I pushed her guts back into the tear in her stomach, then held the werewolf pelt over the gaping wound. I crushed the pelt with both hands, wringing the last of its blood out of the pelt so that it dripped into the open wound. Werewolf blood, with all its regenerative properties. For a moment I couldn't breathe, then the edges of Suzie's wound slowly crept together, and vanished, as though it had never been there at all.

The pelt crumbled and fell apart, and I threw it away. It had done its job. I sat Suzie up again and cradled her in my arms, rocking her slowly back and forth. Her breathing became stronger, and more regular, and suddenly her eyes snapped open, wide and questioning. For a moment she just breathed steadily, as though it was a new thing and not to be trusted, and then her bloody hands went to her stomach, where the wound had been. Finding nothing, she looked at the unmarked flesh for a while. Then she smiled tremulously and turned her head back to look at me. I nodded and smiled, and she smiled back.

She slowly raised one hand and touched my face with her fingertips. I sat very still, afraid to do anything that might break the moment. Her fingertips moved slowly, hesitantly, across my cheek, my lips, delicate as the breath of a butterfly's wing. And then she pushed herself away from me, almost throwing me away. She knelt on all fours, with her back to me, breathing heavily and shaking her head back and forth.

"Suzie . . ." I said.

"No. I can't *do* this!" she said, in a voice so harsh it must have hurt her throat. "I *can't*. Not even with you."

"It's all right," I said.

"No it isn't! It'll never be all right. No matter how many times I kill him."

She rose unsteadily to her feet, looked around for her shotgun, and snatched it up from the floor. And then she shot Belle in the face three times, until there was hardly anything left above the neck.

"Just in case," said Suzie. "Besides, look what the bitch did to my best jacket."

I got to my feet and looked at her resolutely turned back, and for once in my life I didn't have a damned clue what to say. There was the sound of hurrying feet outside in the corridor, and Suzie and I both turned quickly to face the door. I think right then both of us would have been happy to see Walker with reinforcements. We could have used something to hit. But it was only Razor Eddie, appearing abruptly in the open doorway with his pearl-handled straight razor in his hand. He saw Belle's body, and relaxed a little.

"Where the hell were you?" said Suzie, lowering her shotgun.

"It will take more than a three-storey drop to kill me," said Eddie, in his pale ghostly voice. "But there's a limit to how fast even I can take three flights of stairs. Still, you seemed to have coped quite well in my absence. Where's Walker?"

"He made himself scarce when the trouble started," I said. "No doubt he'll soon return, with backup."

"Someone's coming," said Eddie. "I can feel it. Someone's coming, but it isn't Walker."

And we all looked round sharply as we suddenly realised we weren't alone in the office any more. Standing by the desk was a grey man in a grey suit. Up close, even his face looked grey. The angels had found me.

"Get out of here, John," said Razor Eddie. "There are more coming. Lots of them." He moved forward to put himself between the angel and Suzie and me. "Move! I'll hold them off."

He raised his left hand, and in it was the Speaking Gun, poisoning the air with its presence. The angel began to glow, a light so bright it seemed to come from another place entirely. Suzie and I ran for the open door. We clattered down the stairs at full speed, a terrible pressure building on the air behind us. It felt like a storm was coming. It felt like thunder in the blood, and lightning in the soul. We hit the lobby together and kept running. And from far away and close at hand, we heard the awful sound of a single backwards spoken Word. Something screamed, so loudly I thought my head would burst. Suzie and I ran out into the street and kept going, and the whole damned warehouse exploded behind us. The shock wave almost blew us off our feet, but somehow we kept going, and didn't stop running until we were at the end of the street.

We finally stumbled to a halt and looked back, breathing harshly. The walls of Big Sergei's Warehouse collapsed slowly inwards, and disappeared in a great outrushing of black smoke. In a moment, there was nothing left of the building except a great pile of rubble.

"Think Eddie got out in time?" said Suzie.

"I think so," I said. "Razor Eddie's always been very hard to kill."

"Isn't that what they used to say about Belle?"

"We'd better get moving," I said. "More angels will be on the way."

"Terrific. Where can we go that will be safe from angels?"

"Strangefellows," I said, trying hard to sound confident. "I've got an idea."

"Oh, that's always dangerous."

"Shut up and run."

SEVEN

Manifesting Merlin

Suzie Shooter and I ran through the Nightside, with Heaven and Hell close behind. Angels circled overhead in a narrowing gyre, riding the night skies on widespread wings, closing in remorselessly as Suzie and I sprinted down one deserted street after another. The night was full of fires and explosions, death and destruction. All the power and sleazy majesty of the Nightside, brought low in a single night, crushed under celestial heels. I looked quickly about me, trying to get my bearings. I didn't know the warehouse district that well, and I was so turned around now that the only thing I was still sure of was that I was a long way from home and safety. I chose another street at random and plunged down it, Suzie pounding away at my side. I had a stitch in my side that was killing me, and she wasn't even breathing hard.

Something moved in the street ahead, and I stumbled to a halt. Suzie saw it too, and crashed to a halt just ahead of me, automatically bringing her shotgun to bear. Two dim figures came running down the street towards us, silhouetted against the fires burning behind them. They both looked . . . wrong, somehow. And then the skin of Count Video came flapping down the street, raw and empty, with his flayed body running weeping after it. Suzie and I drew back to let them pass. There was nothing we could do.

"I don't think the city resistance is faring too well," I said, trying hard to sound calm.

"Just when you think you've seen everything . . ." said Suzie. "These angels are hard-core. We have got to get off the street, Taylor. But I am fresh out of ideas. Think of something. Fast."

From up above came the sound of great wings, beating on the night. Hundreds, maybe thousands of them, sounding lower all the time. I glared about me, looking for inspiration. We had the street pretty much to ourselves. Everyone else had either gone to ground or was waiting to be buried under it. Dark, hulking, anonymous buildings lined the street to either side. Some of them were more damaged than others, but none of them had lights in their windows. Suzie and I were on our own, surrounded by the enemy, and miles and miles from friendly territory. Business as usual, really, only more so. And just when things couldn't get any worse, they did.

Grey figures appeared out of nowhere, blocking off the street ahead of us. A dozen grey men in grey suits, watching us, unnaturally still and focussed. I looked behind me, and, sure enough, there were more grey figures there. The angels had found us. I looked up at the sky, half-expecting to see winged figures plunging down, to snatch us out of the street and carry us away, but there was no sign of any attack. Presumably they thought we still had the Speaking Gun. Once they figured out we didn't, we were dead in the water.

The figures up ahead pulsed suddenly with a bright and brilliant light, pushing back the night. Suzie and I both cried out, dazzled, and had to raise our arms to shield our faces. We'd grown too accustomed to the gloom. Widespread wings blazed like the sun. I looked back, eyes smarting, only to see grey figures disappear inside a sea of darkness that rolled slowly up the street towards us. A complete and unrelenting shadow, far darker than any mere absence of light could ever be. Unbearable light ahead, and a merciless dark behind.

"Oh shit," said Suzie.

"My thoughts exactly," I said. "Please don't shoot at the angels, Suzie. If you do, and they notice, they'll get even more annoyed with us."

"What do you mean us, white man?" Suzie flashed me a brief smile. "These bastards really do want you, don't they, Taylor?"

"They want my gift, my ability to find things. Whichever side controls that is pretty much guaranteed to get to the Unholy Grail first."

"Well," said Suzie, "given that we are outclassed, outnumbered, and almost certainly out-gunned, might this be a good time to strike some kind of deal?"

"No," I said immediately. "I don't work for free. And I don't trust extremes, of whatever kind."

"I really don't think they're in the mood to take no for an answer."

"And there is the very real possibility that either side would be willing to destroy me, rather than lose my gift to the enemy." I looked at Suzie. "They only want me. You could . . ."

"No I couldn't," said Suzie. "I'm not leaving you. That much I can do for you."

The light swept slowly down the street, while the darkness advanced from behind. It would have been a close bet which was the most disturbing to look at. Such pure manifestations didn't belong in the material world. And I really didn't want to be still standing here when the two forces met. I looked about me while Suzie hefted her shotgun unhappily.

"All this, just for you, Taylor? Haven't these creeps ever heard of overkill?"

"They're angels, Suzie. I think they invented the

concept. Remember Sodom and Gomorrah? And we're facing agents from Above and Below . . . The light and the dark, and us caught right in the middle."

"Story of my life," Suzie said briskly. "Come on, Taylor, I'm waiting. What are we going to do? What can we do?"

"I'm thinking!"

She sniffed. "You always did freeze in the clinch, Taylor."

Suzie turned her shotgun on a recessed door in the wall beside us and let fly with one blast after another, as fast as she could work the pump. The door collapsed and blew inwards in a cloud of smoke and splinters, blown right off its hinges. Suzie dived through the jagged gap into the gloom beyond, with me crowding her heels all the way.

Once inside, we moved to either side of the open doorway and pressed our backs against the wall, while we waited for our eyes to adjust to the dim light. The wall felt comfortably thick and solid, even though I knew it wouldn't even slow the angels down. I felt as much as saw a huge, echoing space before and around me. A little light came through slit windows set high up on the walls, and I began to make out a series of narrow aisles between towering stacks of piled-up merchandise. Outside in the street, inhuman voices rose in rage and frustration. The sound was pure and primal and painfully loud. The two forces swept down the street and slammed together with a sound like mountains crashing. The floor shook underfoot, and the walls of the warehouse trembled. Flashes of blinding light flared through the slit windows, illuminating the warehouse like lightning going to war. And above it all, the sound of giant wings beating furiously. The air was heavy with significance, with the feeling of vital matters being decided by forces far above Humanity. I snorted, and shook my head. Like I was going to let that happen. *This is the Nightside, you bastards. We do things differently here . . .*

"Any idea where the hell we are?" said Suzie. "All I can see is crates, and all I can smell is sawdust and cat's pee."

"If we're where I think we are, they manufacture lucky charms here. Let's hope some of it will rub off. This way, I think."

I pushed myself away from the wall and strode off into the gloom, Suzie padding along beside me. We threaded our way through the piles of stacked crates, heading for the far end of the warehouse. We hadn't made twenty feet before what was left of the doorway was blown inwards by a blast of concentrated light. The gloom was banished in a moment, every part and content of the warehouse thrown into sharp relief. I ran like hell, and Suzie was right there beside me. The floor shook under our feet like an earthquake as angels punched through the warehouse wall like it was made of paper. I put my head down and kept running.

The floor broke open right in front of me, a jagged crack that widened in an instant into a gaping crevice. I tried to jump it, but didn't even come close. My stomach lurched as my kicking feet found nothing beneath them, and I fell into a darkness that seemed to fall away forever. At the last moment I caught the far edge of the crevice with one flailing hand, and fastened on to it with a death grip. My shoulder exploded with pain as my fall was suddenly halted, all my weight hanging from the one arm. I scrambled for the edge with my other hand, but I couldn't quite reach. The ground was still shaking, and the edge under my hand didn't feel at all secure. I looked up, and there was Suzie, on the far side of the gap, looking down at me. I should have known she'd make it. She knelt, studying my situation, her face entirely blank.

"Get out of here," I said. "They don't want you. And I think I'd rather fall than let them use me."

"I can't let you fall, Taylor."

"You can't touch me, remember?"

"Hell with that shit," said Suzie Shooter.

She reached down with one hand, and I reached up with my free hand and grabbed it. Suzie's face set into cold, determined lines, and her grip was as sure as death, sure as life, sure as friendship. She hauled me up out of the crevice, and we both fell sprawling on the far side of the gap. She let go of me the second I was safe, and we both scrambled to our feet on our own.

"You'd be surprised what I can do, when I have to," said Suzie.

"No I wouldn't," I said. "I've tasted your cooking, remember?"

Sometimes humour is all we have to say the things that can't be said.

Angels came crashing through the warehouse wall as though it was nothing more than heavy mist. As though the angels were more solid, more real than anything in the material world they currently moved in. And perhaps they were, at that. Brilliant light and pitch-darkness invaded the warehouse, consuming everything they touched. Suzie glared at me.

"Tell me you've come up with an idea, Taylor. Any idea. Because I think we've run as far as we're going."

"I do have an idea," I said. "But I'm reluctant to use it."

"It's a wonderful idea," Suzie said immediately. "Whatever it is, it's a marvelous idea. I am in love with this idea. What is it?"

"I have a short cut that can take us straight to Strangefellows. Sometime back, in a weak moment, Alex Morrisey gave me a special club membership card, for use in emergencies. Once activated, the magic in the card will transport us right into the bar.

Alex heard about a rather unpleasant experience I had with the Harrowing, outside his club . . ."

Suzie was staring at me ominously. "You've had it all along, and you haven't used it?"

"There's a catch."

"Why am I not surprised?"

"Magic like this leaves a trail," I said patiently. "The angels will know immediately where we've gone. I was still hoping we might shake them off . . . but that doesn't seem to be an option any more."

"Use the card," said Suzie. "Trust me, this is the right time to use it. Morrisey's always boasted his place had major-league protections. I say it's well past time we put that to the test."

"He won't be pleased to see us."

"Is he ever? Use the card!"

I already had it in my hand. A simple embossed card, with the name of the club in dark Gothic script, and the words *You Are Here* in blood red lettering. I pressed my thumb against the crimson words, and the card activated, thrumming with stored energy. It leapt out of my hand and hung in mid-air before me, pulsing with light and bubbling with strange energies. Alex always liked his magics showy. The angels sensed what was happening, and both sides surged forward. The card grew suddenly in size and became a door, which opened before me. Comfortable light and convivial sounds spilled out into the warehouse. Suzie and I ran through the opening into Strangefellows, and the door slammed shut behind us, cutting off the frustrated screams of thwarted angels.

I suppose I must have made more impressive entrances into Strangefellows, but I can't think when. Certainly the two of us appearing out of nowhere, crying *Run for your lives! The angels are coming!* made one hell of an impression. The crowd of assorted suspects and dubious types drinking in the club all suddenly remembered they had urgent appointments somewhere else and left the bar in an extreme hurry. Some used the doors, some used the windows. A few vanished in impressive puffs of black smoke, while others opened their own doors to less immediately threatening locations, and disappeared into them. One thoroughly panicked shapeshifter turned himself into a barstool, and hoped not to be noticed. And one guy (there's always one) took advantage of the general confusion to vault over the bar top and make a grab for the cash register. But Alex's bouncers, Betty and Lucy Coltrane, got him before he'd taken a dozen steps. Betty took the register away from him, Lucy kicked his arse up around his ears; then they let the dumb bastard run (or more properly limp) away. The Coltranes were both pretty sure they were going to have more important things to worry about. Alex stood behind the bar, watching it all and looking even more bitter and put upon than usual. As the last of his patrons vanished, and the place fell unusually quiet, he threw his mopping-up rag onto the bar top and glared at me.

"Thanks a whole bunch, Taylor. There go my profits for the evening. I knew I should never have given you that bloody card."

Suzie and I leaned on the bar, breathing heavily, and Alex grudgingly pushed a bottle of brandy towards us. I took a good swallow, then passed the bottle to Suzie, who drank the rest of it. Alex winced.

"Why do I even bother giving you the good stuff? You never appreciate it. Now what's this about angels coming here?"

"They're right behind us," I said. "And in a really bad mood."

"Tell us this place is protected," said Suzie, wiping her mouth with the back of her hand. "I really need to hear this dump is seriously protected."

"It is protected," said Alex. "But possibly . . . not *that* protected."

"Be specific," I said. "What have you got?"

Alex sighed heavily. "I hate giving away trade secrets, but . . . Basically, this whole building is protected by wards, shaped curses and genetic-level booby-traps laid down by various magicians down the centuries, all of them pretty powerful and vicious as all hell. Grandfather put a really nasty curse on people who miss the urinals in the toilet. And, of course, my ancestor Merlin's still buried somewhere under the wine cellar. More than enough to keep the flies off, even in the Nightside, but no-one ever said anything about bloody angels! I don't suppose anyone ever thought the possibility would arise. Of course, they didn't know about you, Taylor."

"You could always turn me over to the angels," I said. "I'd understand."

"This is my bar!" Alex snapped immediately. "No-one messes with my patrons, even if it's you. And no-one tells me what to do in my own bar, not even a bunch of celestial storm troopers. Should I lock all the doors and barricade the windows?"

"If you like," I said.

"Won't it help?"

"Not really, no."

"You're a bundle of fun to be around, Taylor, you know that?"

Suzie had her back to the bar, her shotgun in her hands, glowering warily about her. "Taylor, how long before the angels get here?"

"Not long," I said.

"Am I at least allowed to ask why both of you are soaked in what looks revoltingly like fresh blood?" said Alex. "Not that I care if you're hurt, of course. I ask only for information, in the interests of hygiene."

"I met up with an old friend," I said.

"Anyone I know?"

"Belle."

"Oh," said Alex. "Her. Is she . . . ?"

"She rests in pieces."

"Good," said Alex. "Snooty bitch. Never liked her. Always putting on airs and looking down her nose at my bar snacks. And she always ordered the best champagne and never paid for it."

"You wouldn't happen to have a really, really big gun stashed away behind your bar, would you?" Suzie said hopefully.

Alex sneered in her face. "Even if I did, I'm not stupid enough to annoy an angel by pointing it at him. Anyway, last I heard, you and Taylor had the Speaking Gun . . . Tell me you still have the Speaking Gun."

"We lost it," I admitted.

Alex really looked like he was about to have a fit. His fists clenched, his teeth clenched, and he actually shuddered for a moment with frustration and outrage. He grabbed two tufts of spiky hair sticking out from under his beret and tugged at them dangerously.

"That is typical of you, Taylor! As long as I thought you had the Speaking Gun, I thought we might actually have a chance. But no! You get your hands on one of the most powerful weapons in the Nightside, and you lose it! You're a jinx, Taylor, you know that? You are nothing but bad news, and always have been! I can feel one of my heads coming on . . . How are we supposed to defend ourselves now? Buy the angels a round and spike their drinks? Lucy, Betty, emergency measures! Right now!"

The Coltranes fell to with a will, moving all the
furniture away from in front of the bar, and opening
up a large clear space. (The shapeshifted barstool
yelped quietly at the rough handling, but refused to
turn back.) Once the Coltranes had created a big
enough space, they laid out a large pentacle, using
salt cellars from behind the bar to mark the lines.
They made a really professional job of it, considering
they were drawing it freehand. Bouncers have to
know many special skills, especially in the Nightside.
We all took our places inside the pentacle, then Lucy
and Betty sealed and activated the design by scrawl-
ing disturbing signs in the vales between the five
points. Betty drew the last sign with a flourish, and
the salt lines blazed with blue-white energies. Properly constructed pentacles drew their power from ley
lines, the living nervous system of the material world.
Unfortunately, angels drew their power from somewhere even more impressive.

Betty and Lucy Coltrane sat down together and
held each other tightly. They'd done all they could.
Suzie and I stood back-to-back, watching and waiting. Alex muttered darkly to himself while trying to
look in all directions at once. At least when he wasn't
shooting dark glances at me that clearly said *This is
all your fault. Do Something. And you'd better have a
really good plan.* As it happened, I did. But I wasn't
going to tell him about it just yet. Because he really
wasn't going to like it.

Upstairs, the front door to the club blew in. There was the sound of great wings beating, followed by the tread of heavy feet. A blindingly bright light spilled out of the foyer but stopped abruptly at the top of the stairs leading down into the bar proper. A heavy tension built on the air, oppressive and threatening like a storm about to break, as the angels pressed against Strangefellow's ancient defences. All of the windows shattered at once, vicious shards of glass flying through the air, only to fall just short of the pentacle's glowing lines. A blackness far darker than the night oozed through the windows, swallowed them up, then crept slowly across the walls.

"They're here," said Suzie. "Heaven and Hell."

"And poor Humanity caught in the middle, just like always," I said. I turned to Alex. "And now, it's up to you. We need your ancestor, Alex. We need Merlin."

"No," he said. "No way. I won't do it."

"He's the only one powerful enough to make a stand against angels, Alex."

"You don't know what you're asking, John. I can't do it."

"That's your big plan?" said Suzie. "Call up Merlin? What's he but another dead sorcerer who won't lie down?"

"According to some Arthurian legends, his full name was Merlin Satanspawn," I said. "Because his father was supposed to be the devil."

"Just when you think things can't get any worse . . ." Suzie scowled unhappily. "I can see a rock and a hard place moving into position around us. If you like, I could just shoot us all now. It might be less painful."

"Relax, Suzie," I said. "I'm on the case. Alex . . ."

"Don't make me do this, John," he said quietly. "Please. You don't know what it's like, what it does to me. When I call him up, he manifests through me. He takes my place in the world. I have to cease to exist, so he can be real. It feels like dying."

"I'm sorry, Alex," I said. "Really. But we don't have the time for me to be kind."

I pushed my gift into his head, found the connection that still existed between Alex and his most ancient ancestor, and pushed it hard.

"Merlin Satanspawn; come forth!"

Alex cried out, in pain and shock and horror, and ran out of the pentacle before any of us could stop him. He got as far as the bar before the change hit him. The whole world seemed to shudder, as reality shifted and changed . . . and where Alex had been, suddenly someone new, or rather very old, came into the world. He sat in state upon a great iron throne, the heavy black metal carved and scored with crawling, unquiet runes. He was naked, his corpse-pale body decorated from throat to toes with curving Celtic and Druidic tattoos. Many were unpleasant and actually disturbing to look upon. Between the ancient designs, his skin was blotchy and discoloured and visibly decayed in places. He'd been dead a long time, and it showed. His hair was long and grey, falling past his shoulders in convoluted knots, and stiffened here and there with clay and woad. Upon his heavy brow he wore a crown of mistletoe. His face was heavy-boned and ugly, and two fires leapt and danced in the sockets where his eyes should have been. There was an ancient wound in the centre of his chest, where skin and muscle and bone had been torn apart, leaving a gaping hole. His heart was gone, torn out, long and long ago. He was Merlin, dead but not departed, powerful beyond hope or sanity. Merlin, sitting on his ancient throne and smiling horribly.

They say he has his father's eyes . . .

He only still existed through an awful act of will. Life and death and reality itself bowed down to his magics. Though there were those who said he was only still around because neither Heaven nor Hell would take him.

"Who disturbs me at this time?" Merlin's voice was deep and dark, and grated on the ear like fingernails dragged across the soul.

"I'm John Taylor," I said, politely. "I called you. Angels have come to the Nightside, from Above and Below, in search of the Unholy Grail. They threaten this place, and your current descendant."

"Damn," said Merlin. "If it isn't one thing, it's another."

A voice spoke from the top of the stairs; a choir of voices speaking in a harmony so perfect it was inhuman. "We are the Will of the Most High. We are the soldiers of the shimmering plains, and the Courts of the Holy. Give us the mortal, for we have need of him."

Another voice spoke, from out of the darkness that had enveloped the windows and was spreading slowly across the walls. Its harmonies were dissonant and disturbing, but still inhumanly perfect. "We are the Will of the Morningstar. We are the soldiers of the Pit, and the Inferno. Do not stand in our way. The mortal is ours."

"Typical angels," said Merlin, sitting utterly at ease and unmoved on his iron throne. "All bluff and bluster. Bullies, then and now. The Hereafter's attack dogs, only with less manners. Guard your tongues, all of you. I am the Son of the Morningstar, and I will not be spoken to in such a fashion. I could have been the Anti-Christ, but I declined the honour. I was determined to be free, from both Heaven and Hell. I gave birth to Camelot, and the song that never ends. I made a Golden Age for Mankind, an Age of Reason. And then the Holy Grail came to England's fair shores, and no-one could think of anything else. They all went riding off on their stupid quests, abandoning their duty to the people. And, of course, it all fell apart. What is Reason, in the face of dreams? I still miss Arthur. He was always the best of them. Arthur, my once and future King."

"Did you really get to see the Holy Grail?" said Suzie, who would interrupt anybody. "What was it like?"

Merlin's smile softened, just for a moment. "It was . . . wonderful. A thing of beauty, and of joy. Almost enough to be worth losing the world for. Almost beautiful enough . . . to shame me for the shallowness of my vision. Man cannot live by Reason alone."

"And now the Unholy Grail's come here," I said. "I've been told it would be a really bad thing if either set of angels gets their hands on it. Judgement Day was mentioned, and not in a good way."

"The sombre chalice . . ." Merlin raised one rotting hand to the gaping hole in his chest. "I suppose it was inevitable the ugly thing should turn up here. The Nightside was created to be the one place where neither Heaven nor Hell could intervene directly. A place apart, free from the tyrannies of fate and destiny. In the Nightside, even the Highest and the Lowest can only work through agents. Which is why the angels are so much weaker here."

Suzie and I exchanged a glance. If these were angels in a weaker form . . . "Excuse me, Sir Merlin," I said, with all the politeness at my command, "Did you just say the Nightside was created for a specific purpose? Who created it, and why?"

Merlin looked at me with his flame-filled eyes, and smiled unpleasantly. "Ask your mother."

Somehow, I'd known he was going to say that.

"If some of these angels are agents of Heaven," said Suzie, in the manner of someone who had a problem bone, and was determined to worry at it until she got an answer that satisfied her, "why have they been killing people, and turning them to salt, and blowing up perfectly good buildings?"

"We only punish the guilty," said the chorused voice in the light. "And so many here are guilty of something."

Suzie looked at me. "They have a point."

"Of course," said Merlin, "here, all the angels are cut off from their Masters. Poor things, they're not used to having to think for themselves. Which is why they've made such a mess. Decision-making isn't really what you do best, is it, boys?"

"We are here for the Unholy Grail," said the light.

"Do you dare stand against us?" said the dark.

"Why not?" said Merlin. "It wouldn't be the first time, would it? Now back off, all of you, or I'll fry your pinfeathers."

The light faded back a little, and the darkness stopped spreading, but the sense of surrounding presences was as strong as ever.

"Taylor," Suzie said urgently. "Tell me there was more to your plan than just this . . ."

"Not even half of it," I murmured. "Hang in there.

Sir Merlin, with your leave I think I can sort out this whole mess in a way that will please . . . well, nobody really, but it'll be a solution we can all live with. *Live* being a relative term, of course. I don't know where the Unholy Grail is, but I'm pretty sure I know someone who does. You see everywhere, Sir Merlin, so could you please grab the Collector and bring him here?"

Merlin gestured languidly with a heavily tattooed hand, and suddenly the Collector was standing right there in the pentacle with us. He looked around, startled, and his eyes all but popped out of their sockets with outrage. He started to say something, then saw Merlin sitting on his throne and shut his mouth quickly before it could get him into even more trouble. The Collector was a podgy, middle-aged man with a thick neck and a florid face, wearing a white jumpsuit and cape, as popularised by Elvis in his later days. It didn't suit him at all.

"Wow," said Suzie, sticking the barrel of her shotgun in the Collector's ear. "Now that's what I call service."

"Oh shit," said the Collector.

"Language!" said Suzie. "There are angels present."

"Hello, Collector," I said calmly. "How's the leg?"

"Taylor! I might have known you were behind this!" The Collector started to say something else, but Suzie shoved her gun a little further into his ear, and he stopped himself again. He glowered at me. "I had to grow a new leg, thanks to your interference all those years ago. Put me right off time-travelling. Never was cost-effective. And besides, I kept bumping into myself, and I kept giggling at me, which was unnerving, to say the least. Now will someone please tell me why I have been transported here against my will!"

"Because you're needed," I said, and then hesitated, because I just had to know. "Is that outfit you're wearing the real thing?"

The Collector pulled himself up to his full, not particularly impressive, height, and preened. It wasn't a pretty sight. "Of course it's real! Graceland hasn't even noticed it's missing yet."

I grinned. "Are you wearing the authentic nappy under it?"

The Collector's eyes narrowed so much they almost disappeared. "What . . . do you want, Taylor?"

"The Unholy Grail. You've got it."

"Yes, and I'm keeping it. The dark chalice is a totally unique piece. It's going to be the pride of my collection. The rest of the collecting fraternity will just die when they hear I've got it!"

"We could all die if we don't get this mess sorted out right now," I said.

"Starting very definitely with you," Suzie growled, applying a little more pressure to the gun barrel in the Collector's reddening ear.

He slapped the gun aside and glared right back at her. "Don't you threaten me, Shooter. I'm protected in ways you can't even imagine."

"Unfortunately, he probably is," I said. "So ease off a little, Suzie. Collector, in case it's slipped your attention, we are currently surrounded by whole armies of angels, all of whom would be quite willing to take you apart, right down to the molecular level, while still keeping you alive and aware and screaming horribly if that's what it takes to get you to hand over the Unholy Grail. Only Merlin's power is holding them back, for the moment. You really think your protections are good enough to hold off a whole bunch of really angry angels?"

He sniffed, but he was visibly weakening. "They don't even know where my collection is."

"It's on the Moon," said Suzie, smiling smugly. "Under the Sea of Tranquility."

The Collector actually stamped his foot, he was so angry, and he waved his pudgy fists in the air. "I knew I couldn't trust Razor Eddie . . . but he had me over a barrel, the bastard. It doesn't matter. Let the angels try and take my prize away from me. They'll discover I can summon up worse things than angels!"

"You're not fooling anyone, little man," said Merlin, and his cold, rasping voice dismissed the Collector's confidence in a moment. "Give up the sombre chalice, while you still can. It's already corrupting your mind."

"It's mine!" said the Collector. "You can't have it! You just want it for yourself!"

Merlin laughed briefly, and everyone winced at the awful sound. "Hardly, little man. I once held the true cup of the Christ in my hands. The Sangreal itself. Nothing less will ever tempt me again."

"I won't give up the Unholy Grail!" the Collector shouted. His face was an unhealthy shade of purple. "I won't, and you can't make me! Not even you, Merlin Satanspawn. Not as long as you still want me to find your missing heart for you someday. Everyone else has failed you. I'm your last hope."

Suzie looked at me, and I sighed. "Okay, very quick précis of a *very* long and complicated story. Merlin lost his heart to a young witch called Nimue, back when the world was a lot younger. She then lost it in a card game. Without his heart, Merlin's power is only a fraction of what it once was. The heart's been through almost as many hands as the Unholy Grail, down the centuries, and is currently . . . missing in action."

"Couldn't you find it for him, with your gift?" said Suzie.

"Perhaps. That's why Merlin's helping us now. Right, Sir Merlin?"

He smiled and nodded, the flames leaping in his eye sockets. What I didn't tell Suzie was that I had absolutely no intention of ever trying to find Merlin's heart. Nobody in their right mind wanted Merlin to regain his full powers. Even dead, he'd be more trouble than the angels . . .

"You can't keep the Unholy Grail," I said bluntly to the Collector. "You don't have anything strong enough to hold off angels, and you can bet they'd be ready and willing to destroy your entire collection, fighting each other over possession of the Unholy Grail."

The Collector pouted sullenly. "They would too, wouldn't they? Bloody winged philistines. All right, you can have it! Ugly damned thing anyway. Merlin? Back to the Moon. Please."

"With a little company, to keep you honest," said Merlin.

I looked at Suzie resignedly. "Hang on to your aura," I said. Suddenly Suzie and I and the Collector were somewhere else.

EIGHT

Cats and Robots and One Last Vicious Truth

Every time I get teleported anywhere, I end up watching my whole life flashing before my eyes. Or at least, edited highlights. Most of it seemed to make some kind of sense at the time. I live in fear that someday Someone will find a way to slip in commercials.

Suzie and the Collector and I materialised out of nowhere, surrounded by thick clouds of noxious black smoke. Merlin learned his magic in the Old School, and still believed in traditional effects. Suzie batted at the smoke with her hand, swearing harshly in between racking coughs, while I checked to make sure I still had two of everything I should have. You can't be too careful with other people's teleport spells. Hidden extractor fans soon sucked most of the black smoke away, and we were able to take a clear look at our surroundings. We'd arrived in an almost blindingly technicolour reception area, with bright hanging silks for walls, dyed in every colour of the rainbow, and twice as gaudy, while thick chequer-board padding covered the floor and the ceiling. My feet sank deeply into the cushioned floor, and walking across it I rose and fell so suddenly that I almost felt seasick. The air smelled strongly of something very like pine. Suzie glared about her suspiciously, the shotgun in her hands, but there were no obvious threats.

The Collector brushed aside one hanging silk to reveal a small high-tech console, all gleaming steel and crystal displays. He stabbed at the controls with his podgy fingers, ignoring everything else, while muttering something to his console that sounded suspiciously like *Daddy's home*. I was more concerned with the fact that I couldn't see a door anywhere. Suzie finished her coughing by hacking up what sounded like half a lung, and then spat viciously on the padded floor.

"I wish Merlin would get over his need for flashy special effects," she growled. "That smoke always plays hell with my sinuses."

"Boys and their toys," I said. "We have to allow

Merlin his little eccentricities. Because if we don't, he'll probably turn us into frogs. Collector, what are you doing?"

"Shutting down some of my internal security systems," he snapped, without looking round. "I have all kinds of hidden protections here, and I don't want them all opening fire on you the moment you enter my warehouse. Some of my collection might get damaged. I have to be careful. There are always people trying to break in and steal my precious things. Bastards!"

"The nerve of some people," I murmured. "Thinking they could steal some of the many things you've stolen."

The Collector said nothing, still hunched over his console. I bounced a few times on the padded floor, checking my weight. If we really were somewhere under the Sea of Tranquility on the Moon, someone had gone to a lot of trouble to make things feel like home. The gravity, air, and temperature all seemed perfectly normal. Which suggested that the Collector must have a lot more high-tech hidden away somewhere else. Suzie prowled restlessly back and forth in the confined space, poking at the hanging silks with the barrel of her gun. She jabbed at the padded floor with one bootheel and sniffed loudly.

"I always said you belonged in a padded cell, Collector."

"I believe in being comfortable and indulging myself," he said, finally turning away from his console. "The padding is there to protect me in the event of sudden, unexpected fluctuations in the artificial gravity. Most of the tech that keeps this place running comes from a possible future I visited, and I have to admit I'm not fully sure how all of it works. I know which buttons to push, but the minute anything goes wrong, I have to fall back on trial and error. Mostly I let my robots run things. You'll meet them later."

"That's the trouble with looting," I said. "There's so rarely enough time to grab the instruction manual as well."

"I do not loot! I collect and preserve!"

"So where is this famous collection?" said Suzie. "Don't tell me we came all this way to hang around what looks suspiciously like a tart's boudoir? We are on something of a tight schedule, remember?"

"Right through here," said the Collector, a little sullenly. "Follow me."

He ducked past a deep puce hanging silk and opened a concealed door. He gestured for Suzie and me to go first, but neither of us was having any of that. We made him go first, then followed quickly on his heels as he led us into the biggest damned warehouse I have ever seen. It seemed to stretch away forever, the walls so far off I couldn't even see them. There was no ceiling, just a bright unfocussed glow from somewhere up above. And filling this gigantic warehouse; thousands upon thousands of wooden crates, in every size you could think of. They were stacked in towering piles, each marked with a stencilled number. Narrow aisles ran between them. I looked around, trying to get some idea of the size of the collection, but the sheer number of crates numbed my brain. There was nothing on display, nothing to admire or examine. Just crates.

"This is *it*?" said Suzie, wrinkling her nose.

"Yes it is, and *don't touch anything!*" the Collector said severely. "I've shut down the hidden guns, but my robots are still programmed to protect my collection from any and all harm. I may have to allow your presence for a while, but that's as far as I'll go. You're here for one object only, and I will get that for you. Luckily I was only just packing it up when Merlin grabbed me. I can see I'm going to have to upgrade my security again."

"Somehow, I'd always pictured something more impressive," said Suzie. "Don't you ever put any of the good stuff out, so you can play with it?"

The Collector winced. "It's much safer this way. I don't encourage visitors, and for me, owning an item is everything. All right, when I first obtain a piece, I do get a certain satisfaction out of holding it, examining it, enjoying all its many qualities . . . I do like to examine every detail . . . close-up . . ."

"If he starts to drool, I may puke," said Suzie, and I had to nod in agreement.

The Collector scowled at both of us. "*But,* once the

initial thrill is over, I immediately pack it safely away in here. It's the thrill of the chase I really enjoy. That, and the knowledge that I've done my rivals dirt, that I've got my hands on something, and they haven't. I do so love to crow and preen in all the best newsgroups . . . And, of course, everything is computerscanned before it's put into storage, so I can visit it again at my leisure in virtual mode. After all, some of the more delicate items aren't up to too much . . . handling. And it's so much easier to find an item on a computer menu than try to dig through all this lot looking for one particular item."

That was when the first of the robots made its appearance, and Suzie and I immediately lost all interest in what the Collector was saying. The metal figure came striding down the narrow aisle towards us on impossibly slender legs, a tall and spindly thing of shining steel and brass, its clean lines the very definition of art deco. It advanced on us smoothly, unhurriedly, its every movement impossibly graceful. The robot was vaguely humanoid in shape, though the squarish head had been cast to resemble a stylised cat's features, right down to jutting steel whiskers and glowing slit-pupilled eyes. The long-fingered hands ended in vicious claws. More robots appeared silently out of the many interconnecting aisles, until we were faced by a small army of cat-faced automatons. I thought I could detect a faint humming from them, so high it was only just in the range of my hearing. They seemed to be talking to each other. The Collector smiled on them fondly. Suzie's shotgun moved restlessly back and forth in her hands, seeking a target.

"Relax, Suzie," said the Collector. "They're only looking you over. Getting used to your presence. Strangers make them nervous. I had them programmed that way. Nothing like a spot of paranoia to keep a guard on his toes. I picked this lot up in a particularly good deal from another possible future. They have basic limited AIs, built around polymerised cat's brains. Simple, obedient, and marvelously malicious when they have to be. They do so enjoy a good chase . . . and the torture afterwards. The purr-fect protectors for my collection. They built this whole place for me and run it in my absence. Far better than any fallible human guards, and besides, I don't care for company these days. I prefer to be alone, with my things. My lovely things."

"No offence, Collector," said Suzie, "but you are seriously weird, even for the Nightside."

"For someone who wasn't trying to offend, I thought you did awfully well," I said.

"Is all well, master?" said one of the cat-faced robots, in a thrilling female contralto that made Suzie and me look at the Collector in a whole new way.

"All is well," the Collector said grandly. "You may all return to your regular duties. My guests will not be staying long. I'll call if I have need of you."

"As you wish, master," said the robot, then they all

turned smoothly on their steel heels and disappeared back into the many narrow aisles of the warehouse. Suzie watched carefully until they were all gone, then turned back to the beaming Collector.

"Do they all have to call you master?"

"Of course."

"Doesn't that get creepy after a while?"

"No. Why should it?"

"Don't go there, Suzie," I said. "We really don't have the time."

The Collector led the way down a narrow aisle that to the untrained eye looked exactly like all the others, and Suzie and I followed after him, pulling faces behind his back. We stuck close; the hundreds of interconnecting passageways made up a maze it would clearly be only too easy to get thoroughly lost in. I let my eyes drift over the many crates and cases we passed; a few were labelled as well as numbered. One label said *Antarctic Expedition 1936; Do not open till the Elder Ones return.* The exterior of the crate was covered in frost, despite the uncomfortable warmth of the warehouse. A much larger crate was labelled simply *Roswell 1947.* It had air holes. Something inside the crate was growling, in a thoroughly pissed off way. And one crate standing on its own levitated proudly a few inches off the floor. I don't know what was inside that crate, but it smelled awful. Suzie drew my attention to a smaller box that was juddering fiercely, almost shaking itself apart. I tapped the Collector politely on the shoulder, and indicated the box.

"What the hell have you got in there?"

"Perpetual motion machine," said the Collector. "Can't figure out how to turn the damned thing off."

"You have so much amazing stuff here," I said. "Who do you share it with? Who else gets to see all the marvels and wonders you've acquired?"

"No-one, of course," he said, looking at me as though I was crazy.

"But . . . doesn't half the fun of collecting lie in showing off your treasures to someone else?"

"No," said the Collector firmly. "It's all to do with ownership. With knowing it's mine, all mine. I do like to rub my rivals' noses in it, now and again; show them proof that I have some hotly contested item that we've all been after. I drive them crazy with jealousy, then laugh in their faces. But in the end it wouldn't matter to me if no-one knew what I had but me. It's enough to know that I've won. That I'm the best."

"That's all this is?" said Suzie. "Whoever dies with the most toys wins?"

The Collector shrugged. "I don't give a damn what happens to any of this stuff once I'm dead and gone. Let it rot, for all I care. I collect because . . . it's what I'm good at. The only thing I've ever been good at. And things . . . possessions . . . can't hurt you. Can't leave you."

For a moment there, he actually looked human, and vulnerable. It didn't suit him.

"Do you want us to keep quiet about the things we've seen here?" I asked.

"Hell no!" he said immediately, all his usual obnoxiousness returning in a moment. "Tell everyone! Drive them mad with curiosity and envy! My problem has always been that I can't prove how big my collection is without bringing people here to see it, and, of course, I can't do that. They'd only betray me and try to steal something. There are people who've spent their whole lives plotting how to get in here . . ."

"You weren't always the Collector," I said. "I've seen photos of you, with my father, from when you were both younger. What were you . . . before this?"

He looked at me, not bothering to hide his surprise. "I thought you knew. I worked for the Authorities, along with Walker and your father. Protecting the Nightside. We were all such friends, in those days. We had such plans, such hopes . . . but in the end it turned out we all had different plans and different hopes. I retired, before they could fire me, and set up on my own. One day I'll own the whole damned Nightside. And then I'll make them listen to me."

I was so fascinated by what he was saying and its implications that I didn't notice all the robots sneaking up on us. Suzie did. Nothing gets past her. She realised I was mesmerised by the Collector's hints and allusions, and elbowed me firmly in the ribs. I looked up and found we were surrounded by ranks and ranks of the the cat-faced robots, standing perfectly still and silent, watching coldly with their glowing cat's eyes. There were hundreds of the damned things. The Collector realised that I'd finally noticed and stopped talking in mid sentence to laugh cheerfully in my face. He was well out of reach, and I had more sense than to try and make a grab for him. The robots looked decidedly . . . menacing.

"I had to keep going until enough of my boys arrived," he said, almost giggling with self-satisfaction. "You didn't really think you could see my collection and my home, with all its secrets, and live, did you? To hell with Merlin, and the angels; nothing can touch me here. I'm protected by spells and tech beyond your imagination, and Merlin won't catch me napping twice. The Unholy Grail is my greatest prize, the jewel of my collection, and I won't give it up! I'll never give it up! I'll just stay here, safe on the Moon, until all this nonsense has blown over. And long before then, you'll be in no condition to betray my secrets to anyone. Perhaps I'll have what's left of you stuffed and mounted. Something to brighten up the reception area."

"You'd kill the son of an old friend?" I said.

"Of course," said the Collector. "Why not?"

He gestured to the waiting robots, and they surged forward in perfect unison. Suzie opened fire with her shotgun, blasting robots as fast as she could work the pump action. The robots shattered under the bullets' impact, flying apart in showers of steel and brass shrapnel that had us all ducking for cover. Suzie kept firing, grinning fiercely as robots blew apart before her. Either she'd found a whole new kind of ammunition for her gun, or they didn't build robots to last in the future.

It helped that the narrow aisles meant the robots could only come at us a few at a time. Suzie and I put our backs to the wall of crates, while the Collector danced back and forth in the background, crying out miserably as some of his crates were inevitably damaged or destroyed by the exploding robots. Suzie pulled grenades from her belt, and lobbed half a dozen where they'd do the most good. Robots and crates blew apart in bowel-churning explosions, and for a while it seemed to be raining machine parts. The Collector cried out for Suzie to stop, and when she didn't, he ran from crate to crate, prying them open and looking inside, searching for some weapon or device he could use against us. He didn't seem to be having much luck. Suzie reloaded the shotgun from her bandoliers and went back to blowing robots apart like metal ducks in a shooting gallery. She was grinning widely now, her eyes hot and happy.

But the robots kept pressing forward, forward, and there didn't seem to be any end to their numbers. The Collector must have got a job lot. One of them got close enough to take a swipe at me with a clawed hand, and I decided enough was enough. This far from the Nightside, I didn't have to worry about the angels seizing my soul again. So I opened my third eye, my private eye, and used my gift to locate the automatic shutdown commands in the robots' minds. I knew they had to be there. The Collector didn't trust anyone, not even his own creatures. He had to have a way to shut down the robots in case they ever turned against him. I hit the commands I'd found in those clever polymerised cat's brains, and all the robots froze suddenly in mid motion. A few of them had got worryingly close. Suzie slowly lowered the smoking shotgun, took a deep breath, and turned to look at me.

"You could have done that at any time, couldn't you?"

"Actually, yes."

"Then why did you wait so long!"

"You looked like you were having fun."

Suzie considered that for a moment, then smiled and nodded. "You're right. I was. Thank you, Taylor. You always did know how to show a girl a good time."

"All vicious gossip, rumours and lies," I said. "Collector . . . Collector? Where are you?"

We found him not far away, slumped exhausted and weeping over another open crate. Whatever it held was buried in plastic packing pieces. The Collector stirred them miserably with one hand, then looked up at us. He spat at me, but his heart wasn't in it.

"Look at what you've done . . . so many lovely things destroyed . . . It'll take me weeks just to find out how much I've lost. Bullies, both of you. No respect for art, for the treasures of centuries . . . And I have weapons here! Great weapons, that would stop even you! I have the Horn of Jericho, Grendel's Bane, even the legendary lost Sword of the Daun. But I can't find them!"

"Show us the Unholy Grail," I said, not unkindly. "The sooner you hand it over, the sooner we'll be gone."

The Collector nodded a few times, sniffing back tears, and finally dug his hands deep into the packing pieces before him.

"I was packing it away when Merlin grabbed me. It is my greatest prize, but . . . the dark chalice is too disturbing to have around. The air's always cold, the shadows have eyes, and I hear voices, whispering . . . things. Ah. Here."

He brought out a small beaten copper bowl, gleaming dully in the subdued lighting. It was dented and dull and not at all impressive. We all looked at it for a long moment, then the Collector offered it to us. I hesitated to touch the thing.

"That's *it*?" said Suzie. "*That*'s the dark chalice, the Unholy Grail? The cup Judas drank from at the Last Supper? That miserable-looking thing?"

"What were you expecting?" said the Collector, smiling just a little at one last chance to show off his expertise. "You thought perhaps it would be some great silver chalice, studded with jewels? Romantic medieval claptrap. The Disciples were a bunch of poor fishermen. This is the kind of thing they drank out of."

"It's the real deal," I said. "I can feel it from here. It's like every bad thought you ever had, wrapped up in one never-ending nightmare."

"Yeah," said Suzie. "Like it's poisoning the air, just by existing."

The Collector looked at me slyly. "You could keep it for yourself, Taylor. You could. This simple cup is powerful beyond all your wildest fantasies. It could make you rich, worshipped, adored. It can satisfy every dirty little yearning in your soul. It has the answer to every question you ever had. The truth about your past, your enemies . . . even your mother."

I looked at the Unholy Grail, and it was like looking into the heart of temptation. Suzie watched me carefully, but said nothing. She trusted me to do the right thing. And in the end, perhaps it was that trust that gave me the strength to turn away.

"Put it in a bag, Collector. I wouldn't dirty my hands by touching it."

The Collector pulled an airline carry-on bag out of the packing pieces and stuffed the Unholy Grail into it. He almost seemed relieved. I took the bag and slung the strap over my shoulder.

"Merlin!" I said, raising my voice. "I know you're listening. We've got it. Bring us home."

Merlin's magic gathered about us, preparing to teleport Suzie and me back to Strangefellows, and the waiting angels. And in the last possible moment, when the Collector was sure the teleport spell had been activated and couldn't be stopped, he stepped forward and shouted one last vicious hurt.

"You're not the only one who can find things, Taylor! There was a time I used to take commissions, in return for help in establishing my collection. I found your father for your mother! I put them together. Everything you are is because of me!"

I went for his throat with furious hands, but Suzie and I were already fading away. The last thing I heard on the Moon was the Collector laughing, loud and bitterly, as though his heart would break.

NINE

For the Remission of Sins

Strangefellows sprang into being around us again, and Suzie braced herself for the thick black smoke, but there wasn't any this time. She looked suspiciously about her, and there was Merlin, no longer sprawled on his dark iron throne but leaning casually against the long wooden bar, a bottle of the good whiskey in one tattooed hand. He smiled unpleasantly and took a long drink from the bottle. I glanced at the gaping hole in Merlin's chest, where his heart used to be, half-expecting to see the swallowed whiskey come running out of it.

"Welcome back, far travellers," said Merlin. "In

deference to your delicate feelings, I dispensed with the smoke this time. Typical of youngsters today. No respect for tradition. Probably wouldn't know what to do with a newt's eye if I slapped it in your hand."

I stepped forward, and he stopped talking. "Send us back!" I said, my hands clenched into fists, so angry it was all I could do to get the words out. "Send us back, right now. Better still, grab the Collector again and haul his nasty arse back down here, so I can beat the truth out of him with my bare hands."

"Easy, tiger," said Suzie, moving in close beside me. Her voice was surprisingly gentle. "I'm the violent one in this partnership, remember?"

"Things change," I said, not taking my eyes off Merlin. "I want the Collector here, right now. He knows things. Things about my mother, and my father. And I will break his bones one by one, and make him eat every last piece, until he tells me what I need to know."

"Wow," said Suzie. "Hard-core, Taylor."

"I'm sorry," said Merlin, still leaning against the bar, entirely unmoved by the raw fury in my voice and eyes. "The Collector has disappeared from his lair under the Moon's surface, taking his collection with him. I can't see him anywhere. Which ought to be impossible, but that's the modern age for you. No doubt I'll track him down eventually, but that will take time. For a mere mortal, he's surprisingly elusive."

I was so angry and frustrated I could hardly breathe, ready to lash out at anyone, even Merlin. Suzie moved as close to me as she could without actually touching me, calming me with her presence, and slowly the red haze began to lift from my thoughts. It's always thoughts of family that drive me crazy, and it's always my friends who bring me back.

"Let it go, John," Suzie said calmly, reasonably. "There'll be other times. He can't hide from us forever. Not from us."

"And now it's time for me to go," said Merlin. "You have the sombre chalice in that bag. I can feel its awful presence from here. I can't be this close to it. Too many bad memories . . . and far too much temptation. I may be dead, but I'm not stupid."

"Thanks for your help," I made myself say, in an almost normal tone. "We'll meet again, I'm sure."

"Oh yes," said Merlin. "We have unfinished business, your mother and I."

And before I could pursue that any further he was gone, disappearing back into his ancient grave somewhere deep under the wine cellar. The arrogant bastard always had to have the last word. Reality flexed and shuddered, and Alex Morrisey was suddenly back among us again, sitting slumped in the middle of the pentacle. He groaned loudly and shook his head slowly. He realised he had a bottle of whiskey in his hand and took a stiff drink. He almost choked getting the stuff down, but he was determined.

"I should have known he'd get into the good stock," he said bitterly. "Damn. I hate it when he manifests through me. My head will be full of corrupt Latin and Druidic chants for days." He shuddered suddenly, unable to continue with his usual facade. He looked at me, and I knew that behind his ubiquitous shades, his eyes were full of betrayal. "You bastard, Taylor. How could you do that to me? I thought we were friends."

"We are friends," I said. "I know that can be difficult, sometimes. I'm sorry."

"You're always sorry, John. But it never stops you screwing up people's lives."

I didn't say anything, because I couldn't. He was right. He struggled to his feet. I offered him a hand, but he slapped it aside. Lucy and Betty Coltrane moved quickly in and got him on his feet again, supporting him between them until his legs were firm again. He looked at the airline bag slung over my shoulder and gestured jerkily at it with his whiskey bottle.

"Is that it? Is that what you risked my sanity and soul for? Get the damned thing out and let me take a look at it. Haven't I earned the right? I want to see it."

"No you don't," I said. "It's vile. Poisonous. Your eyes could rot in your head just from looking at it for too long. It's dark and it's evil and it corrupts all who come into contact with it. Just like its original owner."

Alex sneered at me. "You always were a frustrated

drama queen, Taylor. *Show me.* I've a right to see what I suffered for."

I opened the airline bag and took out the copper bowl, holding it carefully by the edges. It was feverishly hot to the touch, and my skin crawled at the contact. It felt as though someone new had entered the bar, someone terribly old and horribly familiar. Part of me wanted to throw the thing away, and part of me wanted to clutch it to my breast and never give it up. Alex leaned forward for a better look, but didn't try to touch it. Just as well. I wouldn't have let him.

"*That's* it?" said Alex. "I wouldn't serve a cheap claret in that."

"You're not going to get the chance," I said, trying to keep my voice normal. I stuffed the bowl back into the bag, though the effort brought beads of sweat to my brow. "This nasty little thing is going straight to the Vatican, where hopefully they will have the good sense to lock it up somewhere extremely safe, until the End of Time."

"If only it was that simple," said Walker.

We all looked round sharply as the Authorities' chief voice in the Nightside came strolling unhurriedly down the metal stairs into the bar. He still looked every inch the city gent out on his lunch break. Calm and sophisticated, and very much the master of the moment. He glanced at the pitch-darkness filling the bar's shattered windows, but didn't seem in the least perturbed by it, as though he saw something like it every day. And perhaps he did. This was Walker, after all. Alex scowled at him.

"Perfect. What the hell are you doing here, Walker? And how did you get in?"

"I'm here because the angels want me to be here," said Walker easily, striding across the floor to join us and stopping just short of the pentacle's salt lines. He glanced at it briefly and looked away, managing to imply that he'd seen much better workmanship in his day. Walker could say a lot with a look and a raised eyebrow. He tipped his bowler hat to us and smiled pleasantly. "The angels contacted the Authorities and made a deal, and the Authorities sent me here to implement it. And while this club's defences are more than adequate to keep out the usual riffraff, they're no barrier to me. I have been empowered by the Authorities to go wherever I have to go, to carry out their wishes. And right now, they want the Unholy Grail. They intend to hand it over to the angels, in return for . . . certain future considerations. And an end to all violence and destruction in the Nightside, of course."

"Which set of angels?" I asked.

Walker shrugged and smiled charmingly. "Yet to be determined, I believe. Whoever makes the better offer. I understand it could go either way. Still, that isn't really any of your business, is it? Give me the Unholy Grail, and we can all get on with our lives again."

"You know that isn't going to happen," I said. "Angels can't be trusted with the dark chalice, and neither can the Authorities. None of you have Humanity's best interests at heart. So, do you think you can take it from me, Walker? I don't see any backup, this time. Are you really ready to go head to head with me?"

Walker looked at me thoughtfully. "Perhaps. I'd really hate to have to kill you, John. But I do have my orders."

Suzie pushed past me suddenly, standing at the edge of the pentacle so she glared right into Walker's face. "You set your pet on me. Set Belle on me. I could have died."

"Even I just have to do what I'm told, sometimes," said Walker. "However much I might regret the necessity."

"Wouldn't stop you doing it again, though, would it?"

"No," said Walker. "My position doesn't allow me to play favourites."

"I ought to shoot you dead where you stand," said Suzie, in a voice that was cold as ice, cold as death.

Walker didn't even flinch. "You'd be dead before you could pull the trigger, Suzie. I told you, I'm protected in ways you can't even imagine."

I moved quickly to stand between them. "Walker," I said, and something in my voice made him turn immediately to look at me. "There are things we need to talk about. Things you should have told me long ago. The Collector had some very interesting information about the old days, when you and he and my father were such very close friends."

"Ah yes," said Walker. "The Collector. Poor Mark. So many possessions, and none of them enough to make him happy. Haven't talked to him in years. How is he?"

"Well down the road to full on crazy," I said. "But there's nothing much wrong with his memory. He still remembers finding my mother, and putting her together with my father. If the three of you were as tight as he says, you had to know all about it. So who commissioned him to go out and find my mother, and why? What part did you play in it all? And how come you never told me anything about this before, Walker? What else do you know about my parents that you've never seen fit to share with me?"

By the end I was shouting right into his face, almost spitting out the words, but he held his ground, and the calm expression on his face never once changed. "I know all kinds of things," he said finally. "Comes with the territory. I told you all you needed to know. But there are some things I can't talk about, not even with old friends."

"Don't just think of us as old friends," said Suzie. "Think of us as old friends with a pump-action shotgun. Tell him what he needs to know, Walker, or we'll see how good your precious protections really are."

He raised a single eyebrow. "The consequences could be very unfortunate."

"To hell with consequences," said Suzie. Her smile was really unpleasant. "When have I ever given a damn for consequences?"

And perhaps he saw something in her eyes, heard something in her voice. Perhaps he knew Suzie Shooter's shotgun wasn't just any shotgun. So he smiled regretfully and used one of his oldest tricks. The Authorities had given him a Voice that could not be denied, by the living or the dead or anything in between. When he spoke in that Voice, gods and monsters alike would bow down to him.

"Put down the shotgun, Suzie, and step back. Everyone else, stand still."

Suzie put down her gun immediately and stepped back from the edge of the pentacle. Nobody else moved. Walker looked at me.

"John. Give me the bag. Now."

But what was in the bag burned against my side like a hot coal, fanning the anger within me, feeding the fury that blazed within me. I could feel the power of the Voice, but it couldn't get a hold on me. I stood my ground and smiled at Walker, and for the first time his certainty seemed to slip a little.

"Go to hell, Walker," I said. "Or better yet, stay right where you are while I come and beat the truth out of you. I'm in a really bad mood, and I could just use someone like you to take it out on. Can you still use the Voice when you're screaming, Walker?"

I stepped out of the pentacle, crossing the salt lines,

and nothing could touch me. I could feel myself smiling, but it didn't feel like my smile at all. I was ready to do awful things, terrible things. I was going to enjoy doing them. Walker backed away from me.

"Don't do this, John. To attack me is to attack the Authorities. They won't stand for that. You don't want them on your trail, as well as your enemies."

"Hell with you," I said. "Hell with them."

"That isn't you talking, John. It's the Unholy Grail. That's why you're shielded from me. Listen to me, John. You don't know how much I've done to protect you, down the years, using my position in the Authorities."

I stopped advancing on him, though part of me didn't want to. "You protected me, Walker?"

"Of course," he said. "How else do you think you've survived, all these years?"

"Oh, you'd like me to think that, wouldn't you? But I know better. You belong to the Authorities, Walker. Body and soul. And now you're scared, because the Voice they gave you doesn't work on me. Perhaps it's the Grail, perhaps it's something I inherited from my mother or my father. You tell me. Are you ready to talk about my parents now?"

"No," said Walker. "Not now. Not ever."

I sighed, shrugged the airline bag off my shoulder, and let it fall onto the floor. Something cried out, in shock and rage, or maybe that was only in my mind. I stirred the bag with the toe of my shoe, and sneered at it. I'm my own man, now and always. I looked at Walker. "Why is it that everyone seems to know all about my parents except me?"

"The truth is, no-one really knows it all," said Walker. "We're all just guessing, and whistling in the dark."

"You're not getting the Unholy Grail," I said. "I don't trust you."

"Me, or the Authorities?"

"Is there a difference?"

"Now that was cruel, Taylor. Quite unnecessarily cruel."

"You hurt Suzie."

"I know."

"Get out of here," I said. "You've done enough damage for one day."

He looked at me, then at Suzie and the others, still standing rigidly inside the pentacle. He nodded to them, and they all relaxed as the paralysis disappeared. Walker nodded once to me, then turned and walked briskly out of the bar and back up the metal steps. Suzie dived for her shotgun, but by the time she had it levelled he'd already disappeared. She scowled at me, her lower lip pouting in disappointment.

"You let him go? After everything he did? After what he did to me?"

"I couldn't let you kill him, Suzie," I said. "We're supposed to be better than that."

"Well done," said the man called Jude. "I'm really very impressed, Mr. Taylor."

We all looked round sharply, and there was my client, the undercover priest from the Vatican, standing patiently by the bar, waiting for us to notice him. Short and stocky, dark-complected, long, expensive coat. Dark hair, dark beard, kind eyes. Alex glared at him.

"Its getting so just anyone can walk in . . . All right, how did *you* get in here, past two sets of homicidal angels and my supposedly state-of-the-art defences that I'm beginning to think I wasted a whole bunch of my money on?"

"No-one can prevent me from going where I must," Jude said calmly. "That was decided where all the things that matter are decided. In the Courts of the Holy."

"You aren't just an emissary for the Vatican, are you?" I said.

"No. Though the Vatican doesn't know that. I want to thank you for bringing me the Unholy Grail, Mr. Taylor. You've done me a great service."

"Hey, I helped," said Suzie.

Jude smiled at her. "Then thank you too, Suzie Shooter."

"Look," I said, a bit sharply, "this is all very civilised and pleasant, but whoever the hell you really are, how do you intend to get the Unholy Grail past the supernatural brigades surrounding this place?

They've already destroyed half the Nightside trying to get their hands on it. How can you keep it from them?"

"By making it worthless to them," Jude said simply. "May I have the cup, please?"

I hesitated, but only for a moment. Bottom line, he was the client. I never betray a client. And he had paid me a hell of a lot to find the Unholy Grail for him. I handed him the airline bag, and he reached in and took out the copper bowl. He dropped the bag on the floor and studied his prize, turning it back and forth. It was hard to read the expression on his face, but I thought it might be a kind of tired amusement.

"It's smaller than I remembered. But then, it's a long time since I last held it," he said quietly. "Almost two thousand years." He looked up and smiled at us all. "My name, in those long-ago days, was Judas Iscariot."

I think we all gasped. None of us doubted him. Alex and the Coltranes retreated to the far end of the pentacle. Suzie turned her shotgun on the client. I stood my ground, but I could feel a terrible chill creeping through my bones. Jude. Judas. Of course I should have made the connection . . . but you don't expect to encounter two Biblical myths in one day, not even in the Nightside.

"Taylor," Suzie said tightly, "I think there is a distinct possibility that we have screwed up royally."

"Relax," said Jude. "Things aren't as bad as they

may appear. Yes, I am that Judas Iscariot who betrayed the Christ to the Romans, and afterwards hanged myself in shame. But the Christ forgave me."

"He forgave *you*?" I said.

"Of course. That's what he does." Jude smiled down at the cup in his hands, remembering. "He was my friend, as well as my teacher. He found me and cut me down, brought me back from the dead and told me I was forgiven. I knelt at His feet, and said, *You must go, but I will stay, until you return.* And I've been here, doing penance, ever since. Not because He required it, but because I do. Because I do not forgive me."

"The Wandering Jew," I said softly.

"I've been with the Vatican for years," said Jude. "Under one name or another. Working quietly in the background, doing my best to keep them honest. And now, at long last, I have a chance to purge the last remaining vestige of my ancient sin. Bartender, some wine, if you please."

Outside, the voices in the dark rose in protest. Voices from the light answered them, then the two angelic armies slammed together again, two unimaginable forces continuing a conflict almost as old as Time itself. The whole bar shook, as though in the grip of an earthquake. Jagged cracks opened in the walls, and the dark pulsed at the windows while the light flared in the foyer above. Angelic voices rose, singing battle songs, as they trampled the world beneath their uncaring feet. Jude ignored it all, standing patiently by the bar with his old cup in his hands. Alex looked at me.

"He's your client; you go and get him some wine. I'm not leaving this pentacle."

"It's your bar," I said. "You serve him. I don't think the angels will bother with you now. They sound distinctly preoccupied."

Alex stepped gingerly over the salt lines, and when nothing immediately awful happened to him, he made a run for the bar. He dug at a bottle of house red, pulled the cork, and presented the bottle to Jude with only slightly shaking hands. Jude nodded and held out his cup. Alex poured a measure of wine into it, and Jude made the sign of the cross over it.

"And this . . . is His blood, shed for us all, for the remission of sins."

He raised the cup to his mouth, and drank. And in that moment, the war between the angels stopped. Everything grew still. The darkness slowly withdrew from the shattered windows, and the light faded away from the top of the stairs. Somewhere, a choir of perfect voices was singing something almost unbearably beautiful in perfect harmony. Jude drank the last of the wine and lowered the cup with a satisfied sigh. The song reached a ringing climax, and faded away. There was the sound of great wings beating, departing, fading away into an unimaginable distance.

"They've gone . . ." said Suzie, finally lowering her shotgun.

"They have no business here any more," said Jude. "It's only a cup now. Made pure again, in His name. Blessed, like me."

"So," I said, just a little breathlessly. "What happens now?"

Jude picked up the airline bag and stuffed the cup into it. "I take it back to the Vatican with me, put it on a shelf somewhere, and let it fade into obscurity. Just another old cup, of no particular importance or significance to anyone."

He smiled on us all, like a benediction.

"No charge for the wine," said Alex. "On the house."

Suzie snorted. "Who said the age of miracles was over?"

"You have done all of Humanity a great service," said Jude, bowing slightly to me. "And enabled me to right an old wrong. Thank you. Now I really must be going."

"I hate to spoil the moment," I said. "But . . ."

"The Vatican will pay the rest of your fee, Mr. Taylor. With a substantial bonus."

"Pleasure doing business with you," I said. "Even if it was a little hard on the Nightside."

He smiled. "I think you'll find the angels of the light have repaired all the damage they caused, and put right as much as they can. They are the good guys, after all, if somewhat limited in their thinking."

"What about all the people who got hurt?" said Suzie.

"The injured will be healed and made whole again. The dead, however, must remain dead. Only one man could ever raise the dead to life again."

Suzie walked across the pentacle lines to approach him. Her shotgun was back in its holster. She stopped directly before him and looked him in the eye.

"Are you ever going to forgive yourself?"

"Perhaps . . . When He finally returns, so I can say I am sorry to His face once again."

Suzie nodded slowly. "Sometimes, you have to forgive yourself. So you can move on."

"Yes," said Jude. "And sometimes it was never your fault in the first place."

He leaned forward and kissed her gently. On the brow, not the cheek. And Suzie didn't flinch away.

"Hey, Jude," I said. "Can *you* tell me the truth about my mother?"

He looked at me. "I'm afraid not. Have faith in yourself, Mr. Taylor. In the end, that's all any of us can do."

He turned and walked away, back up the metal stairs, towards the night. At the last moment, Alex called after him.

"Jude, what was He really like?"

Jude stopped, considered for a moment, and then

looked back over his shoulder. "Taller than you'd think."

"God speed you on your way," I said. "But please, don't come back. You guys are just too disturbing. Even for the Nightside."

Simon R. Green, who began his career with Ace quite a few years ago, is now a bestselling author for ROC. He lives in England and writes full-time.